THE ROAD TO LLORONA PARK

THE ROAD TO LLORONA PARK

stories

CHRISTOPHER CARMONA

STEPHEN F. AUSTIN STATE UNIVERSITY PRESS
NACOGDOCHES, TX.

For more information:
Stephen F. Austin State University Press
P.O. Box 13007 SFA Station
Nacogdoches, Texas 75962
sfapress@sfasu.edu
www.sfasu.edu/sfapress

Book design: Tinesha Mix
Cover design: Tinesha Mix
Distributed by Texas A&M Consortium
www.tamupress.com

LIBRARY OF CONGRESS CATALOGING-IN-PUBLICATION
DATA
Carmona, Christopher
The Road to Llorona Park / Christopher Carmona

ISBN: 978-1-62288-117-8

first printing

CONTENTS

The universe is made of stories, not of atoms.

—Muriel Rukeyser

I don't know what any individual should do about crossing her own borders. I only know that I live a happier, more adventurous life, by crossing borders.

—Sherman Alexie

I'm right there, swimming the river of hardships but I know how to swim...

—Jack Kerouac

THE ROAD TO LLORONA PARK

WHAT THE STORY EATS...

I. Under the Bridge

Daniel didn't know what he was doing here. It was almost midnight, and he was waiting by a chain link fence for three kids that were going to show him some old woman who they believe has supernatural powers. Like the Llorona but more Indian. This was insane but what else was he going to do? He was barely holding onto his job, and Nelda wasn't talking to him anymore. He had tried to call her several times since that day and no answer. He had seen her on TV saying she was very sorry for the affair, and she was resigning to be with her family. The usual politician line when they get busted doing what politicians do. The first rule of cheating is don't get caught, and boy did they get caught. But the weird thing was that he really did have feelings for Nelda. It wasn't just the sex. There was something more. Maybe it was the thrill of the affair, but he didn't think so, he still wanted to hear her voice. It didn't help that his dick was all over the internet, so dating for him might not be so easy. It wasn't like he did much dating anyway. He was too busy sleeping with his sources.

"Hey, prensa, over here," a voice pierced the quiet night.

Daniel could see Moises, one of the chicle kids, waving him over to a hole in the fence. Daniel walked over to the hole and saw that it was just Moises and the girl, Tzipora. "Where's Ramses?"

"He not coming. He doesn't like this part," Moises answered as he ran down toward the underbridge.

"Wait, what?" Daniel was confused but if this is what he had to do gain these kids trust then so be it.

Daniel followed them down to where the river meets the bridge and saw a pudgy Indian looking woman sitting with her back against the bridge. She was sitting in front of a fire and next to her was a stack of magazines and newspapers. Moises and Tzipora ran up to her and kissed her on the cheeks and hugged her. They began speaking in a strange language, and they kept looking back at Daniel.

"Moises, is this the woman?"

Moises turned back to Daniel, "Sí, she wants to talk to you."

"Does she speak English or even Spanish?"

"She speaks stories," Tzipora answered.

Moises and Tzipora helped the woman to her feet, and she shambled over to Daniel holding out a copy of today's RGV Gazette. Daniel hesitantly began to reach for the paper, but then a voice pierced the air, "No, don't touch it! It's dangerous."

Daniel stopped short of taking the paper and turned to see Ramses carrying a bamboo stick with duck tape on both ends. "Ramses? What's going on here?"

"Don't take that paper. Come with me. It's not safe."

Daniel took a step back, not knowing what was going on but knowing something was terribly wrong.

Moises and Tzipora began yelling at Ramses in that language again, but Ramses didn't listen. He merely reached his hand out to Daniel and said, "Come on. You don't want to be here."

Just as he was turning to leave, Daniel felt the paper in his hand. He felt a strange sensation travel from his fingers to his feet. Then he could understand what the kids were saying. They were shouting at Ramses to stop interfering. This is what la anciana needs to survive. She needs a storyteller. Then Daniel heard la anciana speak.

"Daniel, I know what you have done," she said, "but I need your help."

Daniel turned and looked at her face, which set him at ease. He wasn't scared anymore. He wanted to hear her out and so he sat down where he was and listened.

She sat down in front of him and said, "I am a storyteller. I come from the world before speaking, and I have lost my way home. I have been trapped here for centuries, and I have fed off of the stories of the land, but lately the stories have dried up. They are fewer now than ever before. They try and fabricate new ones, but they just recycle the old ones with no new vision that makes them stories. I have had to resort to written stories, but those are going away too. So I began to starve, and when these children found me I was so thin I was almost nothing. I was almost dead. But they began to bring me stories. And when that wasn't enough they began to bring me storytellers like liars and criminals. But they weren't really storytellers. I needed a real storyteller. And so they brought me you."

"What can I do?"

"You tell stories. I need that to survive because if I die then the stories of the land will die too and what kind of a world can we have without stories."

"Yes, but what..?"

La Anciana shushed Daniel and leaned forward and whispered, "Daniel, you live for the story. You always have. Now, after all you have been through, you will have to sacrifice for the story. Because you can't let the story starve. It's not in your nature. You must feed the story."

"But what does a story eat?"

La Anciana smiled knowing that Daniel already knew the answer. It only took a second as she opened her mouth. Daniel had never seen anyone open their mouth so wide. He just closed his eyes as the world went dark and then...

II. El Rey de Chicle

It all ended under the bridge. Or at least that was what Rammy's abuela had always told him. 'el puente es donde todas las historias van a morir,' were her exact words and Rammy didn't really know what that meant. He had lived in Los Flores all of his life. All thirteen years of it and for as long as he could remember, his abuela would always tell him that. Maybe because many women spent most of their days with bamboo sticks and Styrofoam cups begging for change from American tourists crossing the bridge. The cup would stick up out of the gap from the chain link fence and the concrete bridge. Abuela had always said that the Mexicans cut that gap so that the beggars could poke their cups through and collect American change. It was a metaphor for U.S.-Mexico relations, she always said.

Rammy's abuela, who's name was Aurelia Garcia del Monte was a proud woman who would never beg. She sold lonches (Mexican street tacos) out of their converted airstream. The truck never had a name of it. Just a sign that read: Lonches 5 for un dollar. Aurelia had been doing this for forty years and had six children during that time. Her husband, Esubio Monte had died on the day after their last child was born: Estrella. From the day she was born, Estrella, was just as cabezona as Aurelia and each day was a challenge raising her alone. At the age of fifteen, Estrella had turned to drugs and ran away from home by the time she was sixteen. By seventeen, she had returned with two twin boys: Ramses and Moises. Ramses was the older brother by two minutes, and he always let Moises know that. When Estrella came home, she did not go to work with her mother but instead went back across the border to work as a criada, and they get occasional letters and money from her.

Ramses got the nickname 'Rammy' because that was Moises' first word and Aurelia was so delighted with that name that it stuck. Rammy was twelve years old when he first saw the old woman under the bridge. At first he thought she was another beggar, but she never came out with the other women. The kids got to calling her "la anciana" because they said she looked like an old india. Rammy never paid her much mind because he was too busy running his chicle business. He wanted to get out of the border and maybe move to the U.S. and go to school and be a real businessman like the guys who cross the bridge every day in their fancy cars, running the maquiladoras. In order to do that, he needed to make some money.

Rammy was known on the streets of Los Flores as El Rey de Chicle. He had five kids working for him: Moises (his brother), Sonia and Alyssa Castro (cousins), Esubio "Ralphy" Sanchez (looked like the kid from the Christmas Story movie because he had a gringo father), and Tzipora Ochoa (girl from next door that wasn't very good but she was beautiful, and Rammy had a thing for her for over a year now). They were a good crew that usually banked around twenty dollars a week, which was good since they only spent five dollars for their entire supply and that lasted them two weeks. At the end of the day, each of the Chicle kids would net about a dollar a day, which was great because they worked every day except Mondays. This was the one day that tourists didn't turn out, so why waste your time?

That was a rule that Rammy had learned from his mentor Tony Perez, the original El Rey de Chicle. Tony was now working for a liquor store running bottles for Texans for tips. He said once you become fourteen you are too old to sell Chicle, you have to move up in the world. Rammy was about to turn thirteen, so he had one year before he had to turn the game over to someone new, probably Ralphy because he was only twelve and he had a good head on his shoulders. For now, this was Rammy's racket, and he ran it well. Tony had taught Rammy everything about slinging chicle but at thirteen, Rammy was outselling what Tony took in by five dollars a week. He ran this racket well and even had time to help out his abuela selling tacos on the weekends.

Rammy didn't pedal the chicle himself anymore, he just managed and made sure the others weren't slacking off. There was a system, and that system needed to run smoothly, or the whole operation would fall apart.

Rammy's gang worked the three-block bridge area where you were likely to get the most amount of tourists. They had to fight hard to keep their territory because the other younger gangs were always looking to try to muscle their way in. Every one of Rammy's gang had a spot they would work, and they would rotate their positions every hour for eight hours so that the same kid wouldn't service area twice in one day. This was effective in getting tourists to buy more than one pack of chicle from the same corner. Sometimes the same corner would sell up to eight packs a day in the same spot to the same tourists. Rammy always kept Tzipora close to him for no other reason than to flirt with her, even though he didn't quite know what flirting really meant. It was because of Tzipora that Rammy went down under the bridge. It was also because of her that he met la anciana, and his life would change forever.

"Rammy," Tzipora whispered to him while he sat on that old black milk carton counting the day's take. "Rammy," she repeated louder this time.

Rammy looked up at her, trying not to lose count and said, "Qué?" then realizing it was Tzipora softened up and said, "Qué paso, Tzi? I don't want to lose count." Rammy liked to practice his English with Tzipora because he wanted to one day go to the States and make his fortune and, as everyone knew, you had to speak English to succeed in America. Plus, he liked Tzipora's accent when she spoke English, he thought it was sexy.

"¡Mirar! la anciana!" Tzipora said.

"La anciana? Really, where?" Rammy said.

"Allá," she said pointing to an old woman shambling down under the bridge. She had one of those old indio blankets draped around her, which was strange because it was September and it was about 100 degrees out.

"I see her. Let me get back to counting the money," Rammy turned back to the money on the milk crate.

"Aye, Rammy, why you always speak to me in ingles?" Tzipora asked, struggling with the last words.

"Because we need to learn it to sell better to los Americanos. It's business, baby," Rammy slipped the last part in hoping she wouldn't notice.

"Why you call me baby? I no baby to you," the words were jumbled, but Rammy knew what she meant.

"Tzipora," Rammy said moving close to her and looking her dead in the eyes, "you are my baby. Mi doña."

"Aye no juegues conmigo, por favor..." Rammy cut her off by kissing her on the lips ever so gently. Tzipora was taken aback by the kiss and blushed... "Rammy," was all she could say sounding as flustered as she was feeling.

"I want you to be my girl, Tzipora," Rammy said sounding as confident as a Don but mentally shaking in his boots on the inside.

Tzipora had always figured Rammy liked her, but she had never heard him say it, and now that he had, she kind of liked it. She also saw an opportunity here. "Rammy, I will be your girl, but," and this is what she learned from her mother who always got men to do things for her because she was beautiful, "I want to see la anciana. Come with me and see where she live."

"Lives."

"Qué?"

"It's lives, not live."

Annoyed, Tzipora said, "Whatever." She had learned that from the young American fresas. "Will you come?"

"Okay, but first a kiss."

Tzipora liked that he was a good businessman and knew how to always negotiate but this time she did want to kiss him. She didn't want him to know she liked it, which is also something she learned from her mother.

Rammy leaned in to kiss her when a voice interrupted them, "Rammy, we are done for today." It was Moises who spoke English with no accent and Rammy hated him for that, but right now he hated him for interrupting his kiss.

"Moises, just leave the money there and go help abuela."

"But Rammy…"

"Moises, just do it."

Moises not knowing why Rammy was so upset put his take on the milk crate with the rest and was about to leave when Tzipora said, "Moises, esperar." She stepped away from Rammy's face and walked over to Moises and said, "Did you want to go see la anciana con migo y Rammy?"

Moises had always wondered about la anciana and wanted to see where she lived so he nodded his head in excitement. Rammy was none too pleased because he had been cock-blocked by his little brother and the worst thing about it was that he knew Moises didn't even know what he had done. Rammy sighed and turned to both of them grinning like idiots and said, "Fine, we will go tonight. Let me finish the count, but go help abuela close up shop. I have to go get mama."

Moises ran off excited, and Tzipora looked over at Rammy and felt sorry for him, but she didn't really know if she felt the same way about him that he felt about her. There was something that stopped her from kissing him back, and she didn't know what it was. But what she did know was that when Rammy was kissing her, she didn't think of Rammy, she thought of la anciana. It was weird; she knew that something about that old india fascinated her, and she needed to meet her. Tzipora watched Rammy count the money and knew that he was upset, so she did something that she learned from her mother as well. She leaned in and kissed him on the cheek. Rammy's tight body relaxed and he felt better, hornier, and more hopeful than before. If finding this old india was what it took to get Tzipora's attention, then he would do it and hopefully after that he would be able to touch her with more than a kiss.

II. Johnny Sancho

This is it. The end. No one likes to talk about that. The end. It's too depressing. When something ends. People like to talk about beginnings. How things start. This is much more inspiring. But the truth is that all things end. And on this day. They ended in a way that I both expected and didn't. Isn't that always the way? We see the end coming even if we don't want to admit it. This may have something to do with our love for beginnings. Or our fear of reaching the finish. Sometimes I wish there were no endings. Just beginnings. Maybe then things wouldn't be so dramatic. No tears. No hurtful words. No crippling depressive thoughts. Just always starting. Something new. Something young. Something without memory. Like a chalkboard freshly erased. No dust. Just a blank slate. But that isn't life. And that is a shame.

Daniel woke with the sun in his face. It always crept in through the cracks in the hotel curtains. They never make them big enough to cover the entire window. He suspected this was done on purpose. Like in hospitals where nurses check in on you every twenty minutes, never letting you sleep. Even when they tell to get some rest. Hotels shouldn't be like hospitals, should they?

"What *time* is it?" she spoke softly. She was the mistake he never should have made. Her name was Nelda Baca and she was a county commissioner for Cameron County. She was also married with three kids and ten years older than him, but Daniel didn't care. He thought she was hot, especially in that black dress she wore last night with those three-inch high black-heeled pumps and no pantyhose.

"What?" Daniel answered not quite awake yet.

"What time is it?" she repeated.

Daniel knew from the light streaming in from the side of the curtains that it had to be early morning. He reached over to check the time on his phone, and the clock read 7:35 am.

"It's early."

Sounding agitated she asked a third time, "No. What time is it?"

"7:30."

She opened her eyes wide and said, "I've got to go."

"No, why?" he said rolling over and looking into her big brown eyes accentuated only the white around her irises.

"Because I'm not even supposed to be here."

"Sure you are."

"Daniel, no, I'm not."

Nelda got up out of bed and at first he didn't realize she was supposed to be naked but she was. She got up, her nipples erect as erasers on No. 2 pencils. It must be the cold air from the air conditioner because she didn't seem like she was turned on. But what did he know? She quickly got her clothes on until all she had left were her shoes. She held those in her by the strap that goes across her heel.

Daniel got up, also naked but very noticeably aroused. You can chalk it up to morning wood if you want, he thought, but he seriously was turned on by how she franticlly put her bra, panties and dress on. Her hair was still a mess, and the remnants of her makeup were just abstract art, but there was a beauty about her that hid behind these perceived imperfections. It was sexy, and he stood up and stopped her before she reached the door. She looked up at him, and her eyes said she didn't want to leave but had to, and his eyes said, "I want you now." Daniel's eyes won the argument, and before she knew it her panties were off, her dress was hiked up, and they were deep into making the headboard slam against the wall.

After about ten minutes she was dressed again and Daniel was laid back in the bed, sweating and spent. She got her shoe on one last time and walked over to the door and said, "Daniel, I will call you."

"With a story I hope."

"You are such an asshole sometimes."

"And you are a bitch, but that is what makes you sexy."

Nelda blushed and opened the door, letting the sunlight blind her for a few seconds and then she put on her sunglasses and took a step out and then walked back in and slammed the door shut hard. She pushed her back up against the wall, and she looked terrified. Daniel sat up and asked, "What? What's wrong?"

She looked at him and everything about her face read fear.

"They got a picture off."

"What? Who got a picture?"

"It's Ceci Molina from the RGV News. She got a picture

off of us."

"How do you know that?"

"Because I saw her take the picture as I was walking out."

"She got both of us? How?"

Then from outside of the door a voice shouted, "Commissioner Baca, I know you are in there with Daniel Ybarra."

Panic gripped Daniel, and he jumped out of bed. He stood facing Nelda, and he knew that she knew. This was the end of both of their careers.

"The story broke Danny. There is not much I can do for you. I have to let you go," Humberto explained.

Humberto Gonzalez was Daniel's editor at the RGV Gazette, the Valley's number 1 paper. "Bert, there's nothing you can do for me? I mean, this is my career, my life."

"Danny, you're sleeping with Nelda Baca, one of our top commissioner's and your top source. Her career is now ruined, not to mention her marriage."

"I know but how many reporters sleep with their sources every day around here."

"Yes, but they don't get caught with pictures. You were naked with a massive erection."

"But she was dressed," Daniel responded.

"Don't try and joke your way out of this. It's over, Danny. I'm sorry but I've got to let you go."

"Bert, come on man, I'm three months behind on my rent. I need money."

"Well, you should have thought about that before you boned the commissioner."

"Let me at least do some stringer work for cash. I will write under a pseudonym."

"Like what Johnny Sancho? And who's going to talk to you anyway? Your face and your pixelated dick are all over the papers."

"Not the real papers, just the internet."

"This is 2005; the internet is quickly replacing us. It's too late. There is nothing I can do for you."

"What about doing a human interest piece? Like promoting some cultural event. They never care who does the reporting there. They just like the positive press," Daniel pleaded.

Humberto sat back in his chair and said, "Okay Johnny Sancho, there is a piece that I have been trying to get someone to cover and so far no takers."

"What is it? I'll do anything."

"You know those chicle kids that hang around the bridge?"

"Yeah, I've bought chicle from them."

"I want to know about them. I want you to write a story about those kids, their lives, all that shit. Since the story's in Mexico, they shouldn't know who you are anyway."

"Thanks, Humberto. I really need this."

"That's all I can do. Do good on this piece and we will see about keeping you on as Johnny Sancho…and oh, don't sleep with any of those kids."

"Ha, very funny."

III. La Anciana

It was dark out, about ten o'clock because the news was on and Aurelia was crocheting in front of the TV. That was the way that she could relax after a long day of making lonches. She knew that Tzipora was over in Rammy and Moises' room, and she wondered what they were doing but not enough to care to get up and check on them. Aurelia knew that Rammy had a crush on Tzipora, but she didn't think the kids were doing anything more than playing. It was late, but it was summer, and the kids didn't have school, so she allowed them to stay up late. Aurelia was usually asleep by the time the sports came on, and she felt that heaviness come over her eyes. The last thing she remembered was a commercial for Sábado Gigante.

Rammy peeked out from the crack in their bedroom door. He had been watching his abuela for about ten minutes now, waiting for her to fall asleep. Rammy knew she would be out by 10:30, but he waited for her snore to make his move. At about

10:35, the snore started quiet and then slow and steady like a lawnmower. Once he heard it he turned to Moises and Tzipora and said, "Ja, she sleeping."

They snuck out through their bedroom window as to not risk waking their abuela. They had with them two flashlights: one for Rammy in the lead and the second for Tzipora. Moises had his trusted walking stick to fight off dogs. The stick was a piece of bamboo duck-taped around both ends to prevent cracking. Rammy had his slingshot in his back pocket just in case of trouble. Things were changing. The streets were getting more dangerous as new gangs were moving in to challenge the established cartels. Rammy, Tzipora, and Moises made their way to the bridge, which wasn't too far from where they lived because Abuela liked to keep her lonche truck close by in case of thieves and also the closer one is to the actual bridge the better the sales.

Tzipora stood on the milk carton that Rammy used to count money to see where la anciana went under the bridge, since this is where she saw her last. "Allí," Tzipora said as she pointed to the spot where she had seen la anciana go. Tzipora jumped off of the crate and started running toward the spot. Rammy and Moises followed her with Rammy yelling, "Esperar!" They chased the bouncing light of her flashlight until they reached the point where there was a fence that stopped them from going down into the river. Tzipora was standing at the fence with her fingers grasping the chainlinks and staring out toward the Rio Grande.

"Tzipora, estas loca. Why didn't you wait for us?" Rammy said between hard breaths.

"¡Mirar, es la anciana!" Tzipora said pointing down where the river met the bridge.

Moises saw her first and clenched his stick tightly. Rammy turned his flashlight toward her, but she was too far for the light to reach her. "Apaga la luz. You will see her better." Rammy did just that after a few seconds of letting his eyes adjust to the moonlight, he saw her. She was sitting with her back against the concrete bridge, and she was eating something, but he couldn't tell what it was. Moises knew what it was because he read that magazine every day. It was Mad magazine. That was how he learned English so good.

"She's eating a magazine," said Moises.

"Qué?" said Rammy, not believing Moises.

"Sí, está comiendo una revista," Moises repeated in Spanish. "She must be starving."

"We should get her some food," said Tzipora.

"We don't know nothing about her. She could be loca. We should go back. We saw her and…"

"…No, we have to help her," Moises said, "porque, if we don't then she will die."

"How you know that? She's old. She's been living here for a long time. I think she will be okay," Rammy said, desperately trying to keep them from going down there.

Tzipora looked over at Moises, who was staring so intently at la anciana eating this month's issue of Mad Magazine, and said, "Let's go help her." Rammy saw the look she had in her eyes and the way she was looking at Moises made him uncomfortable. Moises nodded his head and said, "Sí, let's go." And before Rammy could object, Tzipora and Moises were already making their way down the fence line looking for a hole to crawl through. After about ten feet they found a place where the fence was loose from the fencepost, and they slipped underneath. Rammy followed, upset that Moises was now clearly in charge.

They made it down the steep hill to the riverbank and quickly made their way to the old india sitting at the entrance to the underbridge. Rammy was having trouble keeping up with them and for a second he lost them, but when he thought he would have to start running, he came up upon them. They had stopped running and were looking down at the old india, but more importantly she was looking at them. Tzipora was the first to speak, and she said, "Anciana, estamos aquí para ayudarle."

La anciana responded back in a language they did not recognize, then when she realized they couldn't understand her she held out the last page of Mad magazine and shook it at Moises in a motion for him to take it. He slowly reached for the magazine, and when he did there was a slight flash in his eyes that only Tzipora saw because she was closest to him. Moises smiled and spoke in the same language she was speaking. Rammy took a step back, and Tzipora just smiled. Rammy didn't know what was going on, but he didn't want anything to do with this. Moises took the page from la anciana and held it out to Tzipora. She quickly grabbed it and this time Rammy saw the flash in her eyes and felt scared that something bad was happening to them. "Tzipora, you okay?"

Tzipora responded in that same language, and that sent a sense of dread through Rammy's body. This was some weird brujeria shit here, and he wanted nothing to do with it, but he didn't want to leave Tzipora and Moises with the bruja so, he just shook his head and said, "No, no quiero tocarla, you guys go ahead."

Tzipora turned away from him disappointed and sat down with Moises and spoke in that strange language with la anciana while Rammy stood behind them upset. They spoke for what seemed like hours, and Tzipora and Moises seemed to get closer to each other, which made Rammy even more upset. It was too much for him to take so he finally shouted, "Ja, you've had fun, let's go back, es tarde."

Moises looked back at him and said in English, "Rammy, it's okay. She's a storyteller. She won't hurt anyone. She's just lost."

"Lost? Where she from?"

Tzipora laughed and turned to look at a very upset Rammy and said, "Desde el mundo de cuentos. From the stor-ied world," she said in English.

"Que lengua hablar usted?" Rammy asked.

"Es el lenguaje de la historia," Tzipora answered as if it was obvious.

Even more upset and wanting this to be over Rammy asked, "How we get her back?"

La anciana stood up and walked over to Rammy, who took a step back and readied his fists for defense.

La anciana put her hand out as if asking for change and

said, "I am hungry, Ramses, and I can't eat any more dead stories. I need a living story to be able to get back to my home."

"How we gonna do that?" Rammy shot back with his fists still at the ready.

Moises and Tzipora were beside the old india looking concerned, so Rammy lowered his guard and Moises finally spoke, "We need un otro storyteller."

IV. El Rey del Chicle and Johnny Sancho

The story is alive. It breaths. It eats. And it desires. Like any other living creature, it carries its burden on its back. But what happens when the story gets hungry? Do you feed it or let it starve? What does it eat anyway?

Daniel sat at Garcia's bar drinking his third rum & coke and eating the bar peanuts while watching CNN en español. For the first time in God knows how many years the PRI lost a presidential election and Mexico now has the PAN in power. What that meant no one knew but what was obvious to Daniel was that the winds of change were in the air. The CNN reporter was going on and on about the important change of leadership in Latin America's biggest country. It was barely four months into Calderon's presidency and already things were moving. The border was seeing an uptick in violence. One of the stories that Daniel had been chasing was the sporadic disappearances of people from the U.S. side of the border. It seemed to Daniel that the cartels were losing their hold on the border, and that seems like a good thing at first thought, but then the younger, brasher, more sadistic gangs begin to move in; things only get worse. He downed his drink, paid the bartender, and walked out into the bright sunshine of Los Flores trying to work on a story he didn't care about.

As soon as Daniel hit the street, he scanned the sidewalks for kids selling chicles. He walked around and finally when he was close to giving up for the day, a scrawny kid with a faded Teenage Mutant Ninja Turtle T-shirt and looking very much like that kid Ralphy from Christmas Story came up to him and asked him, "Chicle?"

Daniel smiled, "Sure," he dug into his pockets for loose change and gave the kid fifty cents, "What's your name kid?"

"Ralphy."

Daniel chuckled at the irony, "Really?"

"Sí, Ralphy Sanchez."

"Hey Ralphy, can I ask you some questions? I'm a reporter, and I want to do a story on you kids."

Looking baffled he said, "No hablo ingles, señor."

Daniel dug into his pocket and pulled out a five-dollar bill. "Now, do you speak English?" Ralphy smiled and reached out for the bill, but Daniel pulled it back and said, "First, do you speak English?"

"¿No hablas a español, señor?" Ralphy asked still trying to snatch that five.

"Sí, pero es más fácil para mí en ingles. Soy prensa."

Ralphy smiled, really looking like that kid from *A Christmas Story* and said, "Rammy habla ingles. Ven." Ralphy waved Daniel over as he started to walk back toward a taco truck. But before they got to the truck, they turned toward an alleyway where a young girl was stopping a couple of Winter Birds selling them chicle. Ralphy saw Daniel looking at her and said, "No, aquí." Daniel turned and saw a young boy sitting on a black milk crate counting money and chewing on a red licorice stick. Ralphy ran up to the kid, and they started to talk. The other kid seemed to get irritated, but then he looked over at Daniel, and he calmed down and whispered something to Ralphy, who shook his head and ran back over to Daniel. "Hable con él. He the man," Ralphy said and stuck his hand out for the five. Daniel gave him the five and said, "Who is he?"

"He el rey del chicle. He the man," Ralphy snatched the five and ran back to his position.

Daniel walked over to the dark-skinned kid counting money and looking like a young Jimmy Smits and said, "You're el rey de chicle."

"You can call me Ramses. What do you want?"

"Like I told your boy there, Ralphy, I'm a reporter doing a story on you guys. The Chicle kids."

"Why do you want to do a story on us?"

"Human interest piece."

Rammy didn't quite understand what he was saying to him and showed it on his face.

Daniel continued, "I'm interested in what you do here, you know, help tell your story."

"My story? You want to tell my story?"

"Yeah, might help you sell some more chicles."

Rammy looked him over for a few seconds and then said, "I don't need your help."

Daniel didn't know if he was trying to be tough because he was obviously 'The Man' as Ralphy had so eloquently put it, or there was something else going on here, something more than chicle. "It's quite a racket you got here. You run these kids like a pro," Daniel looked around as several kids kept looking back at Rammy and him talking.

"I do alright."

"Look, kid, I can pay you if that's what you are fishing for."

"I no fish. I don't like prensa in my business."

"I'm not here to burn you kid. I'm here to get your story. To know what it takes to run a chicle ring."

"Not really a story here."

Just then a kid looking like a lighter skinned version of Jimmy Smits ran up to Rammy and his crate and said, "Rammy, I need some more chicle," he looked at Daniel and said, "Who's that?"

"Nobody, he was just leaving."

"I'm a reporter looking to do a story on you kids, would you want to be interviewed?" Daniel said trying desperately to save his story.

Rammy shot him a look that could only read as "I want to kill you now" and turned to the other kid and said, "No."

Moises turned to Rammy and started talking to him in a

language that was clearly not Spanish. Rammy responded back, "No, no more."

Moises seemed agitated, and just then a young girl walked up and started speaking in that strange language to Rammy and Moises. Daniel was completely lost. Were these kids Indians or something?

"Hey, guys, what's going on here?"

After a few minutes of argument between the three of them, Ramses bolted right out off of his crate and said, "Okay. okay. Pero esta es la última vez."

Moises turned to Daniel and said, "Hello sir, my name is Moises, and this is Tzipora…"

"…Tzipora? Is that Aztec?"

Moises looked confused, "No, it's Mexican."

"I was just…never mind. What's going on?"

"My brother, Rammy, he just a little, you know, protecting."

"Protective?"

"Yes, that. Anyway, we have a story for you."

"You have a story for me? What is it?"

"Have you ever heard of La Anciana, the woman who lives under the bridge?"

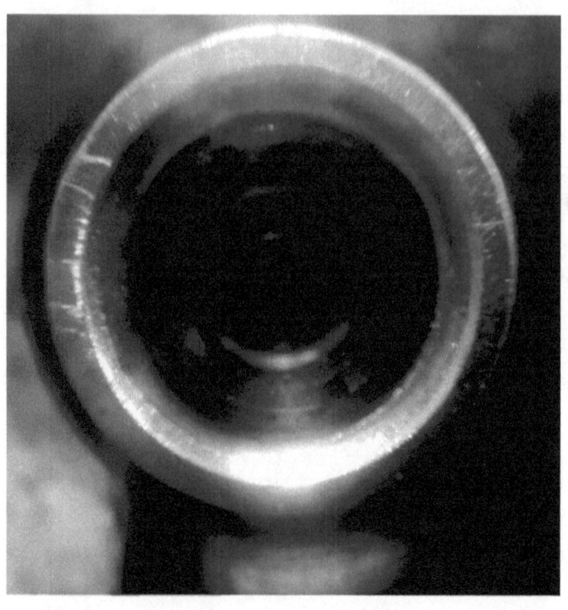

SCENE: *Audition #6*	TAKE: *#1*
DIRECTOR: *Haldon Cruces*	
PRODUCER: *Jaime Garza, James Littleton, and Jorge Quintero*	
DATE: *May 25, 2004*	

THE CUT OF THE FILM

PRODUCTION: Victim of Society

"Hi, my name is Chloe Vela, and I am here to audition for the role of Suzie," said this timid girl as she walked into the room and sat down in the lonely chair across from me and the three shadowy figures behind me.

"Hi, I'm Haldon Cruces, I'm the director on this film, the three gentlemen behind me are the producers of this film: Jaime Garza, James Littleton, and Jorge Quintero."

"Hello," she said.

The minute she walked into the door, I knew she was Suzie,

the murdered teenager girl that the entire film revolved around. The character was written to be a quiet, beautiful, and battered girl. Suzie was abused when she was a child. That was nowhere in the script, but somehow she knew that.

"Do I start now?" she said.

"One second," I said as I pushed the record button on the camera, "Okay, go."

"I don't know what to do, Simon," she started reading her lines with no script in her hand. "He's...he's...hitting me."

"You have to tell someone, a teacher, the cops, someone," I said dryly reading off the script in my hand.

"I can't, he's the Sheriff's son," and at that moment tears streamed from her eyes and I knew she was the one. She was Suzie. She read to the end of the scene never breaking character and never needing a script. She had talent.

Jorge, producer number 3 or as I secretly called him, Moe, piped up as we finished the scene and said, "Can you stand up so we can get a better look at you?"

"Yeah, sure," she said standing up.

"Can you turn all the way around?" that was Jaime, or Larry.

"Very nice, now can you take your sweater off and unbutton your blouse," James or Curly.

I cringed when they ordered her to start to strip in front of us, but I didn't say anything. I merely watched as they ordered to thrust stand profile and puff her chest out and then her ass. Their explanation for this:

"We just want to see how you will look on camera," Moe again, he was the leader of three.

Chloe did everything they asked without complaint.

"Thank you, Chloe, we will be in touch," was all I told her before she left.

She smiled and walked out of the room. The three stooges talked amongst themselves and then said, "I don't know, Hal. I don't know if her tits are big enough."

I turned to look at them and said, "She read the best out of all of them, her breast size shouldn't matter. She'll do great."

Moe leaned forward and said, "Alright Hal, but the chick

that plays her best friend better have big tits."

Curly then interjected, "Let her know that she will have to get naked for this role."

I sighed under my breath and said, "There's no nudity in the script."

"Write it in then," Moe said.

It was an order. They gave out several orders through the making of this film, and many of them were horrible, not just for me, but for the actresses in the film. We auditioned a few more girls and then called it a day.

That night I called Chloe up and told her that she got the part. She was ecstatic, which is a word I hardly ever use but in this case she was. Then I dropped the bomb. "There is a scene where you will have to be topless. Is that okay with you?"

There was a pause that seemed to last forever and then she said, "How much do I have to show?"

I assured her that it would be tasteful and wouldn't just be gratuitous; I lied basically because as much as I wanted this to be true, the stooges wouldn't allow it.

***

I got to know her somewhat throughout the making of this film, Victim of Society, about a guy who shoots the prom king on prom night because he caused the suicide of the girl he was in love with, Suzie. The film was shot in flashback sequence with the interrogation room being the center of the set. Chloe was quiet and reserved but when she got into character she embodied Suzie. Even when I had to add in the sex scene between her and her abusive boyfriend and she had to be nearly naked throughout the scene, she didn't really complain. The stooges wanted her to be totally naked, but I fought them tooth and nail for her to be able to keep her panties on during the shoot. Even as we were shooting the scene, I could hear the stooges claiming the cut away footage from the shoot. It was disgusting, but I grinned and bared it because I was making my movie and that's all that mattered. In between takes I found out she was in college, in drama, and she really wanted to be an actress. She was a lot like the character she was playing. The oldest daughter of a migrant family (undocumented) and besides doing the movie and going to school she worked part time at a call center.

Alright, I'll admit it, I fell for her. Don't all directors fall for their leading ladies? I mean look at Hitchcock, he fell for all of them. He was also a pervert and obsessive. Okay, bad example but anyway, it was hard not to fall for her. She was beautiful, not just physically but inside as well. So I made every excuse to see her off set. Running of lines, test shots, etc. I never made a move on her, though; I always maintained my professionalism. I mean, I was an artist.

The shoot wrapped after about a month, and I set down to edit the film. It was my first feature length film. I had only made short films before this chance, so I knew I had my work cut out for me. I spent two months editing the film together and by the end of it, I had a 2 hour and 20-minute film. Before I cut anything, I had to show it to the stooges. They told me what should be cut, which was not the sex scene, but the some of the dialogue scenes that worked to build character and story. Of course that didn't matter to them. So I cut the film down to just under 2 hours and then invited the cast and crew to view the film.

It was a private screening in the backroom of a taqueria. The whole cast was here, except for Chloe. I was worried she wasn't going to show because since the movie had wrapped, I was planning to ask her out. We had plenty of booze and beer and small snacks. The stooges drank pretty heavily, laughing amongst themselves. I don't know why I took their money. These guys were shady at best. They owned a few strip clubs around the Valley, and they had lots of cash to spend. Larry was a cousin of the lead actor, Jay, who played Simon in the film. Jay loved the script and knew we needed some funding. These guys were willing to flip the bill, but they wanted to be on set to watch us shoot the scenes. I knew they just wanted to watch the girls in the film. It was a compromise that every independent filmmaker has to make, I was told. I am an artist, I constantly told myself.

I wanted to make a socially relevant film, and this was it. Or so I thought.

We started the movie and still no Chloe. About half an hour into the film, my mentor and good friend, Fred Garcia, walked up to me and said, "This is great work. This is what we need. A good Mexican American film about everyday life that doesn't pimp out the culture."

"Thanks, Fred. Just following the Pain Flower example you set," I said praising the film he made ten years ago that was really the first independent film shot in the Valley. That film had not done well, having all of its assets tied up with misspent monies and Austin producers who could never get the film off the ground. But in the Valley, the film was legendary. Fred was the young writer/director behind the project. That was the last film he made before he resigned to teaching at the local community college, but he was still an inspiration to the scene.

Just then Chloe walked in. Fred walked back to his seat and engrossed himself in the film again. Chloe saw me first since I was standing in the back of the room with a clear shot at the door. She wore a black dress with blue flowers and black pumps. She looked really beautiful. She smiled at me, and I walked over to her.

"Glad you could make it," I said.

"Yeah, sorry, I had a photo shoot in Brownsville that ran a little late."

"Oh yeah, hope that went well."

"Yeah, it was good. How is the screening going?"

"It's going well. I hope I didn't screw it up."

"It's a good film."

"You haven't seen it yet. I don't know…"

"…I know it is. Hey, listen, you want to smoke a cigarette with me?"

"Sure," I said. I only smoked American Spirits. She had Marlboro Lights, but that was alright.

We stepped out back in the alley and started talking about dreams and what we wanted from this film.

"I want to be relevant. I want my films to matter like

Matewan or One Flew Over The Cuckoo's Nest," I was babbling trying to sound cool.

"What about Paris, Texas? That was good," she said leaving me astonished.

"You saw Paris, Texas? Wow. I think I love you."

Chloe laughed, and I saw her blush a little. "Yeah, I saw it, and I liked it. I mean it's about a messed up guy running away from his life and responsibilities but that monologue about the fire. That was just so emotional and the fact that he told her this horrible story through a hole in a peep show was just so raw. You know?"

"Yeah, that was great. I never saw it quite that way, but it was cool." I don't know why I did it, but I knew that this was my opportune moment, so I leaned in for a kiss. She met my kiss and returned it and the next thing I knew we were in the backseat of my Chrysler Fifth Avenue my pants around my ankles and her dress pushed up over her stomach. Luckily she had a condom in her purse, so the spur of the moment lovemaking wasn't ruined by going to the corner grocery store and awkwardly buying some over the counter. It was perfect. I didn't know she liked me too, and I was ready to ask her for a proper date.

"So, what are your plans for this film?" she asked.

"Well, I am going to shop it around the festivals and hopefully catch the eye of a distributor."

"What about the producers? Aren't they going to help you find distribution?"

"Who? The stooges? No, they know nothing about the film industry. They love the glamour of it but don't understand the work that goes into making a film or selling it for that matter."

Chloe was silent for a few seconds, and I noticed the air changed from the relaxing post-coital humidity to something a bit colder. "So those guys who produced this film aren't going to be in the selling of the film to Hollywood people?"

I laughed, "No, those idiots only put up the money for the film. This was their first film. No, I'm going to shop it around. Mostly with Fred," I began to feel that there was something behind this line of questions, and I didn't want to know but had to at the same time, "Why do you ask?"

"They lied to me."

This was getting very uncomfortable. "What do you mean? What did you do?" I sat up and pulled my pants up.

Chloe adjusted her dress and slipped her panties back on. We both got out of the car, and she stayed silent.

I repeated, "What did you do?"

"Hal, I really want to be an actress."

"What did you do?" I was livid now thinking she had slept with one of the stooges, "Did you sleep with one of the stooges?"

"Hal, you have to understand that I know how the game is played, and I'm willing to play it."

"What does that mean?"

"They promised me meetings with agents and producers if I only…"

"…if only what? They only wanted to exploit you. They were only interested in seeing you naked. They didn't care about your acting ability or the work. It is all about tits and ass to them. How could you? I thought you were better than that."

"Hal, I know you see yourself as this artist. You have all of these principles, and you see what you do as art, but deep down you know this business is a bit more about tits and ass than art."

I was stunned. I didn't think she thought this way at all. I didn't know what to say to her, "So you prostituted yourself for a chance to be famous?"

"Let me ask you a question, Hal. Seriously, what did you think about me when I came in to audition for you?"

"I saw Suzie. The tortured girl who was the center of my film."

"Come on. If I was short, fat, and ugly would you have cast me? And be honest."

This question stopped me because my initial reaction is that it didn't matter but, "I know that those things shouldn't matter but…"

"…but they do. I know I'm beautiful. I know that I can attract any man I want. I know how to seduce someone just the right way to get what I want. That is something I learned early on when I decided I wanted to act."

It was then that a horrible thought crept into my head, "Did you seduce me?"

Chloe stopped her train of questioning and looked up at me as stone-faced as a statue and said, "Would you have given me the part otherwise?"

I was shocked. First that I ever had feelings for this girl and second that I knew she was right. "I guess you are right, and I guess sleeping with me tonight was about advancing your career, but I really liked you."

"Hal, I really like you too, but I want to be honest here. I am much more interested in jumpstarting my acting career than I am in having a relationship with you. I know that sounds harsh but I'm a player in all definitions of the term, and I am in this game to win."

"Is that what you think this is all about: winning?"

"Being an actress is all I've wanted all my life and so yes, it is about winning. Can you live with that? Because if you can then we can be together."

"But only as long as I can further your career? Right? Because the moment I stop being useful to you, I get dropped. Right?"

"You make it sound so bad. You will get sex out of it in the meantime."

This woman was a great actress. She had convinced me she was an artist and in fact, she was just an opportunist. I felt shook down to my core. "You know, I wanted to be a filmmaker because I wanted to make art. I wanted to create great lines for great actors to give great performances. But you are right. This business is not built on Steve Buschemi's; it's built on Pamela Anderson's. Back in medieval England, they banned theater because they thought it was cover for prostitution and you know what, it is."

"That's a little harsh."

"Says the woman who whored herself out to get ahead."

Her eyes narrowed and she said, "Fuck you, Hal. I am doing

what I have to do."

"You knew they were just checking you out the entire shoot. And you didn't care."

"Of course I knew. I'm not an idiot. But I wanted the part so what's a little tease."

"It can't be this way. There are so many great films for it to be this way."

"Wake up, Hal. This is the world. Either you are in the game, or you are not."

"You keep calling this a game. This is art."

"How many of your principles did you compromise to make your film? I mean, there wasn't a sex scene in this script when I first read it, but then what? The producers asked you to put one in, and you obeyed. Why? For the sake of the film. Right?"

"No…I mean…"

"Be honest. You compromised your film to get it made. That is the business, isn't it? How is that much different than what I did?"

"I got my film made, and you slept with them, and they couldn't even help you," I said with as much vitriol as I could muster. I really wanted to hurt her.

"I slept with you too."

I didn't have a retort for her. I just stood there with my mouth open and my world falling apart. Then I realized something. "You're right. You're right. I can't do this anymore."

I jumped in my car and started it up. I could hear her calling for me, but I didn't respond, I simply drove off. I never saw her or the film again. Not until fourteen years later when I was watching the launching of a new Latino Channel on cable and there she was bikini clad dancing with a bunch of girls under an outdoor beach shower. Or at least I thought it was her, but then I realized that it couldn't be her because this girl was young and Chloe would be well into her thirties. Maybe it was her or maybe it was just another girl trying to be famous too.

THE UNUSED GIFT

There she was standing at my door. I hadn't seen her in 15 years and yet here she was looking a bit frumpier than what I last remembered, but then I guess so was I. It was strange seeing her. We had parted on terms that I could only describe as awkward, and we never spoke, not in 15 years. But there she was, at my front door looking nervous and a little tired around the eyes. Her name is Crystal Benavides or at least it used to be. I invited her in. I knew it was a bad idea, but something inside couldn't turn her away. I needed to know what had happened. What had brought her to my door? But at the same time, my wife would be home within the hour, and I didn't want to bring my past into our home. That time of my life with Crystal was a different me. I was not the same person, but I guess everyone thinks that looking back on life.

Crystal sat down on my plush couch. She was wearing a blue jean skirt that stopped just short of her knees and the way she sat, I couldn't help but look between her legs. It was too dark to see anything with just a glance, but I couldn't help it. I felt embarrassed that I looked, so I looked back at her face, and I could tell she noticed I looked, but she didn't say anything.

"I know this is strange, me coming here out of the blue, after all this time, but I needed to talk to you."

"Okay, do you want some water or something?" I said.

"Sure," she said.

I got up and went to the kitchen and poured her a glass of water and while I am pouring, all of the old memories came flooding back to me. The late nights, the parties, the drugs, and the conversations. Thought I was going to say sex, right? Well, we never had sex, our relationship wasn't like that but, trust me, I have regretted that for years because I learned years later from a mutual friend that she dug me, and I was too hung up on someone else that I didn't even notice. Now, Crystal was beautiful then, thin and big boobed with light brown skin and when she sucked on a straw her tongue would flicker out for just a second. Told you I thought about it. She walked with an elegance that was lacking from most college girls. There was always an air around her that I couldn't explain, but mostly we talked and bonded over poetry and theater. She was an actress; I was a playwright and poet.

I remember when I first met her. I was working as an assistant director on a badly written play by some local celebrity playwright that had one hit play in the '80s and then couldn't write another good play. Well, she played the lead in that, and we often found ourselves talking about good plays, good writing and sharing our mutually bad poetry with each other. I got better or least I hope I did. Anyway, I was fighting with my then girlfriend who eventually turned lesbian. We were having a nasty fight over the phone outside of rehearsal, and I did the one thing you are not supposed to do in a relationship, I hung up on her while she was talking. I immediately regretted it, but it was done. I was on a payphone, so I knew she wouldn't call back. In those days, I carried a pager because cell phones were too big, bulky, and expensive. Everyone carried a pager in those days.

Crystal walked in literally seconds after I had hung up the phone call, and I wore my anguish, my anger, and my regret like cheap cologne. How could I not, it was literally seconds after I had just hung up. I turned and saw her and she said nothing for about a minute. We just stared at each other, and then she said, "Break's over. We are starting again."

"Okay, I'll be right in." I didn't even hesitate. I just went back to rehearsal.

It was after rehearsal when things changed for us. We were packing up, and she came up to ask me if I was okay. I said, "Yeah, sure."

She looked at me, and she knew I was lying. "You want to smoke a joint? I got one in my car."

"Hell, yes."

And so we went and sat in her car, smoking and talking way past midnight. We were the only two cars left in the parking lot, and the sky had turned that color that was edging toward dawn but not quite there. It wasn't sexual at all. I don't know how to explain it except to say that it had nothing to do with sex or attraction in that way. We just connected. Not to say I didn't check her out because I did. I am a guy after all, but this friendship was that, a friendship with pot.

After that night, we were inseparable for what seemed like an eternity. After that night I didn't speak to my then girlfriend, later turned lesbian, for about 2 years. Crystal and I did several plays together, and then I left for Austin, and we never spoke again. I found her on Facebook a couple of years ago, and we friended each other but we never really communicated, until today.

I handed Crystal her glass of water, and she took a big drink like she hadn't drank in days. She set the glass down on the coffee table and looked at me. I was sitting on a couch that was perpendicular to her, so I would always have to turn to my left to speak to her, and I could feel her eyes on me at all times. She didn't say anything for what seemed like hours, but it was only actually about a minute. During that time, I stared at the lipstick stain on the lip of the glass, and I couldn't stop thinking that I would have to clean that before my wife gets home.

"Do you remember the last night we saw each other, Hal?" she said breaking the silence.

"Yes, it was the last showing of our film before I left to Austin."

"I didn't go to the showing."

"I know you didn't. I went to your house and saw you after. What is this all about?"

"I'm dying, Hal."

"What?"

"I'm dying. I have six months tops, the doctors say."

"Oh, I'm sorry. Is it cancer?"

"Do you remember that night?"

"Yes, I do. I called you, but you didn't answer, so I went home."

"And?"

"And you were at my house."

"Did you know how I felt about you, Hal?"

"At the time, no."

"Then why did you call?"

"Because we were friends. I didn't want to leave without saying goodbye."

"Would that last night have happened if you had known how I felt about you?"

"I don't know what you are talking about."

"I'm talking about that night. The night we..." Crystal stopped and started to cough. I got up and got her another glass of water. She drank that one down just as fast as the first. Double lipstick stain.

"Nothing happened that night. I kissed you goodbye, and then you left, and that was that. It was fifteen years ago; we are different people now."

"You don't know anything about me."

"Alright, I'm sorry I don't know you anymore, that's true. You are the one who showed up at my house talking about something that happened a long time ago. I understand that you are sick, and you don't have a lot of time, but what is going on here?"

Things were getting really weird for two people who never had sex. They always say that sex ruins a friendship, but sometimes not having sex ruins a friendship too. There is nothing in this world so powerful as what could have been. It is something that stirs inside of you, thinking about what could have been.

Crystal set her glass on the coffee table and wiped a renegade tear from her cheek. "I'm sorry, this was a bad idea. I just needed…I don't know what I needed."

"Closure?"

"Yeah, closure."

"I don't know why I never made a move. I was young and stupid and thought that friendship was more important than…"

"Sex."

"I was going to say romantic entanglements, but yeah, sex."

"It was a cold night, that night. I remember it like it was yesterday because that night changed everything for me. Do you remember how cold it was, Hal?"

I didn't know where this was going, but I played along, "No, not really."

"It was a strange cold. Maybe because there was a light drizzle and those tiny drops stuck to your skin, never letting you forget that the world is cold. But what happened that night was colder than anything because it was a lasting cold that never left me."

"Crystal, nothing happened that night."

"And whose fault is that?"

"I don't understand."

It was at this point that she dug a small black box with a silver bow wrapped around nice and elegant. If I didn't know any better, I would have thought it was a ring box. She placed it on the coffee table and said, "This is for you."

"What is that?"

"Open it."

"Is that what I think it is?"

"Open it and find out."

"Crystal, this is really getting weird. I'm married, and I

haven't seen you in fifteen years."

"It's not a proposal, just open it."

"I don't know if I should."

"Why? What are you afraid of?"

I picked the box up and looked her right in the eye. I couldn't tell what she was feeling or thinking. Her eyes were just cold and tired. Broken. I looked down at the box and then decided to open it. I slowly pulled the ribbon off and pushed the top of the box back. It snapped open with a click and inside was a single Trojan condom, unopened. Ultra-thin. I didn't know what to think, but luckily she spoke and broke the awkward silence.

"That is what I brought with me that night fifteen years ago. I wanted so bad for us to use it. I wanted to have that movie last-night stand before the star goes off. A night of unbridled passion. But you know what happened that night?"

"Nothing."

"That's right, nothing but a hug and a kiss on the cheek."

"I was young and unconfident. I was filled more with ideals than practicality."

"You should have made a move; I wanted you to."

"Why didn't you?" was the only response I had. It was petty, but it was all I had.

"I asked myself that every day since that night and the only thing I can think of is the same reasons you had, friendship over sex. I thought we would stay in contact, but we didn't, especially after that night."

"I don't understand, you keep talking about that night like it was some life changing event, but nothing happened, and if I remember correctly you stopped returning my phone calls, not the other way around."

Crystal wiped another tear away and said, "Sometimes nothing happening is worse than something happening."

"We seem to be going in circles here, why are you here?"

"Because of that," she said pointing at the box with the condom in it, "I kept it for fifteen years."

"Why?"

"Because that night after I left you, I went to a bar and started drinking, and then I met a guy who I fucked in the backseat of my car, but we didn't use that. We didn't use anything, actually. I was too wasted to even ask him to put one on. And six months later I caught a flu I couldn't shake, so I got tested."

"Oh my god, I'm sorry."

"HIV positive."

I was dumbfounded. "You have AIDS."

"Now I do."

"I thought it wasn't a death sentence anymore."

Crystal shot me a look of anger and said, "That is what most people think, but the life you lead, taking pills and having to explain to anyone you get close to you that you have this disease is not living because they usually want nothing to do with you or worse, they just split. Every cough and sniffle would send them running."

"I'm sorry."

"Stop saying that. What's done is done, right?"

"Crystal, I don't mean to…I don't know what to say."

"That is why I stopped calling. I blamed you for this."

"But why come here, now?"

"I'm dying. My immune system is completely shot."

"Did the medication not work?"

"Oh it works, but I stopped taking it. I'm tired of living this way. No one to love, to make love without precautions."

"You're giving up?"

"You have no right to judge me, not you," she said as she broke down crying with rivers of tears and all I could do was hand her a tissue and sit next to her. I tried to comfort her, but I was the cause of her pain because I didn't make a move fifteen years ago.

"Crystal, you shouldn't give up. There has to be someone out there who doesn't see the disease but sees you."

"Why didn't you make a move? Why? None of this would have happened if you just were another horny asshole."

"I know, but I wasn't. I can't go back and change things."

At that moment, she stopped and looked at me. Her eyes red from crying. Her lips cracked, and her mascara was running.

With a trembling voice, she asked, "If you could, would you?"

I stared at her and wanted to give her the answer she wanted, that I would have slept with her that night and that night would have been so passionate that I wouldn't have left. I would have stayed with her. We would have been married and had kids. I wanted to tell her that but the reality was that night changed things for me too. Because I regretted not making a move that night. I vowed to not hesitate ever again. It was shortly after I moved to Austin that I met my future wife. I didn't hesitate.

So I looked at Crystal, broken and distraught, looking for some comfort in her last days. Looking for the regret in my eyes that something should have happened between us. While I did have regret for the past, it did not control me as it had done to her. So I answered with the only honest answer I could, "I don't know."

La Politiquera

Alejandro Leyva stared at the blinking cursor on his screen hoping that it would inspire words to spill out of him like a flood, but instead it was like that Dutch kid holding his finger in the hole, stopping anything from coming out. He had been working on this novel for over five years now, and he still couldn't find an ending. It eluded him like success in his lifetime. He was thirty-nine years old, and he had just received tenure about twenty minutes ago when his department chair had come into his office and told him that the tenure committee had met and approved his tenure. He was a made man now, but he didn't feel that way. He felt like nothing he had ever done in his life had made a mark on anyone. All he had was this unfinished novel about a political consultant who was trying to find redemption after having lost a major election for a gubernatorial candidate who was given a second chance to work on a city commissioner's race…

knock. knock. knock.

Alejandro looked up from his computer and saw an older woman carrying a Rhetorical Tradition book in her arms with a stack of papers on top. "Dr. Leyva? Can I speak with you?"

Alejandro leaned back in his chair and remembered that these were his office hours, so he said, "Sure, come on in." He didn't recognize her, but she looked like a non-traditional student. He had plenty of those, older folks who come back to school after twenty years or so of being out of school and looking to gain a degree in a world where experience meant less and less compared to a bachelor's degree.

She walked in and placed her books and papers down on his large oak desk. The desk itself was covered in papers and books, so she had to place her heavy books down on top of his.

"I don't know if you remember me," he didn't, "I was in your Argument & Persuasion class last spring. My name is Melly Palacios, but I was Acaña back then. I am divorced."

Alejandro stayed quiet trying to remember her. He looked her over. She had light brown hair, light brown skin, a little on the plump side but still in good shape for a woman in her fifties. "I'm sorry I have several students. I…"

"I know I'm not nineteen and perky like most of your students," she let out a slight chuckle.

"It's not that. I'm sorry, what can I help you with?"

"Well, I need your help. You see, right now there is a County Commissioner seat open because of Nelda Baca stepping down and…"

"You want to run for County Commissioner?"

"Well, no, not me. My daughter Sandra."

"Has she ever run for office before?"

"No, she hasn't, but she really wants this. I think she wants to be a Senator someday."

"Ms. Palacios, I don't know what I can do for you. You need a political manager. I am just an English professor; I can point you to someone that might help, but…"

"I've already been to several people, but I think you can

help us."

"Why is that? I'm not in politics."

"Anymore, but you used to be. In class you talked about working on the Betty Lynch campaign. She was a real contender for governor of Texas and the speeches you wrote for her were inspiring."

Alejandro swiveled his chair to face his stack of books on his shelf and said, "But we lost that race. We lost huge."

Melly leaned forward and touched his arm and said, "But not here. Here she won huge. Look at these numbers. Here in Cameron Country she scored eighty percent of women and fifty percent of men. Even though she was a pro-choice candidate, she still scored big in the Valley. I mean this is Catholic country and she still scored big."

"That's because she was a Democrat. People here in the Valley don't usually vote Republican."

"Yes, that's true but look at these numbers." Melly pulled out a report and slid it across his desk. "These are the numbers before the speeches you wrote for her. She was barely hitting twenty percent and then…" She slid another report across his desk, "these are the numbers after you started writing for her. There was a dramatic surge toward her."

Alejandro swiveled back to look at her, shocked that she was touching his arm. But when he locked eyes with her, he saw a hope and passion that he had not seen since the Betty Lynch campaign. "What kind of experience does she have?"

Melly leaned back "Well, she has worked for me in my store since she was twelve and now she runs her own discount clothing store in the mall."

"What kind of business do you do?"

"My family and I have been in the furniture business for over fifty years. I have been running the two Brownsville stores for twenty-five years."

"Palacios Furniture? That's you?"

"Yes, that's me."

"And your husband? What does he do?"

"Ex-husband. He's a deadbeat. I don't know what he is

doing now."

Alejandro knew he had hit a cord, but he wanted to know how she would hold up to tough questions when the reporters start flinging mud. So he continued, "Why did your husband leave?"

Melly was starting to get upset, and Alejandro saw it. She answered, "Who says he left? I kicked his cheating ass out."

"What about your daughter? What is her relationship with your husband?"

Clearly upset she said, "Ex! Husband! and they talk, and she sees him when he comes around, but I don't see what any of this has to do with my daughter running for county commissioner."

Alejandro sighed and said, "It has everything to do with it because politics, especially here, gets very personal and very mean and if you can't stand up to some tough questions about your marriage, then you will be eaten alive out there."

"But I'm not running, my daughter is."

"I know but you are her manager and her mother, and any dirt you have hidden will come out when these establishment bastards start in on your daughter. Her life. Yours. Nothing will be private anymore."

"But this is just a County Commissioner seat."

"No, ma'am. This is Nelda Baca's seat. That's the seat of power, and everyone knows it. Here in Cameron County that position is as important as President of the United States."

Melly smiled, and Alejandro was caught a little off guard, and she said, "And that's why I want you to manage her campaign."

Alejandro looked her over one more time and then looked back at the blinking cursor on his screen. "When can I meet her?"

Melly, sounding ecstatic, said, "So, you'll do it?"

"Let me meet her first and then we will go from there."

"Oh thank you. You won't be disappointed," she said springing up from her seat and gathering her papers. "How does Friday work? She is out of town right now, but she will be back Friday for sure."

"That works great."

"How does lunch at Dora's sound?"

"Sounds great."

While watching her gather her things, he saw a strand of her hair fall from behind her ear and dangle in front of her mouth. "Do you have plans right now?" Alejandro asked.

Melly stood up and looked at him. "Not really. I was done for the day." This didn't feel business related. This felt like something else.

"Would you like to get some coffee?"

"Sure."

Alejandro shut his laptop and began to stand up. He noticed her struggling with her books and papers and so he said, "You can leave your stuff. The coffeehouse isn't far."

"Sure, okay," she said placing her stuff on his desk again.

Alejandro took Melly to El Corazón de Fuego, the locally-owned coffeehouse which had the best live acoustic music scene in Brownsville. They talked for hours, and he got to learn all about her miserable marriage to a lying and cheating macho asshole and all about her dream of getting an MBA in Business Administration so that she could help her family's furniture business really take off. They had only one store for forty-five years before Melly took over and grew so much business they opened a second store. Alejandro told her about his never being married but being in a serious relationship that lasted twelve years before she moved on to someone else and had three kids. Melly told him about her two children. Sandra, the oldest, and Mario, her baby boy of twenty-two years. It was perhaps the best time Alejandro had in years. For Melly, it was certainly unexpected, but she certainly enjoyed someone's company who wasn't a customer, an employee, or a vendor.

When they stepped out of the café, they realized that it was dark. They had been talking for four hours, and they had not felt it. Alejandro offered her dinner, and she accepted, and they walked over to the little Mexican restaurant down the road and had dinner and drinks. And as they walked back to his office, Melly had her arm hooked through Alejandro's. Her shoes dangling from her hand because she didn't want to walk in heels anymore. They stopped at the Resaca that ran through the university and sat down at the water's edge.

"This is not how I imagined this day would end," Melly said looking out at the moonlight reflecting on the water.

"Is that good or bad?" Alejandro asked, looking at the side of her as she looked at the Resaca.

"Definitely good," she said turning to face him and realizing that his face was only an inch from hers.

"Have I kept you out too late?"

"No, since my son is at UT and my daughter is gone for the next couple of days. It's just me in that lonely house, so no…it is not too late," Melly said as she leaned in and kissed Alejandro.

After a few minutes of kissing, they made their way up to his office, through dark hallways, using only the light from her cellphone to guide them. Alejandro stumbled for his keys, and they both chuckled, feeling like teenagers sneaking back home way after their curfew. Alejandro got the door open and ushered for Melly to enter first. She quickly rushed in and stopped a foot inside because the room was only lit from the outside street lamps that streamed in through the window. Alejandro was about to turn the lights on when Melly said, "No, don't. Lock the door."

Alejandro smiled and moved in to kiss her. Before they knew it, they were completely naked on his desk. Papers and books knocked to the floor. She had her bare legs wrapped around his waist, tiny noises escaping her. It had been a long time for both of them, and they tried to make it last as long as they could.

After they were done, they laid on his office floor using his sport's coat as a blanket. Melly was snuggled against him, her head lying on his bare chest. She just listened to his breathing.

"Wow," Alejandro finally said, "this was definitely not how I expected this today to turn out."

"You already said that."

"Yeah, I know but the statement still stands. How did this happen?"

"I walked into your office and asked for your help with my daughter's campaign."

"Oh yeah, you took my Argument & Persuasion course, right?"

"Well, can I make a little confession?"

"Sure, what is it?"

"I didn't take your class. That's why you didn't remember me. My daughter did."

"Why would you lie about that?"

"Because I thought you would help me if I was a former student of yours."

"I would have talked to you either way; you didn't need to lie."

"I know that now. Are you still going to help us?"

Alejandro looked over at her face. Her eyes were silhouetted by the dim light and said, "I don't want to lie to you, but if I don't think she is a viable candidate then I will tell you that. I don't want you to lose before you are even in the race."

"You mean her. You mean Sandra."

Alejandro looked away from her and said, "Yes, Sandra."

"Friday, then."

"Friday."

"What are you doing tomorrow?"

"Tomorrow I have to go to Matamoros."

"What about tomorrow night then? I would love to see you again."

"Friday. Let's do it Friday."

"Okay, sure."

It was 12:30 pm on Friday and Alejandro checked his watch for the third time. She was late. Sandra Acaña. The new contender for Country Commissioner Seat #14. So far this didn't bode well for her candidacy if she couldn't even be on time for a meeting with her potential new manager. Alejandro checked his phone to see if there were any missed messages but there were none. After about five more minutes, Alejandro decided that she was a no show and flagged down the waitress for his bill. Just then a young woman walked in wearing a gray business suit and pencil skirt looking very much like a younger version of Melly. This must be her, he thought. He still didn't remember her from his classes. He waved her over. "Sandra?" he called out.

She recognized him and smiled and waved back. She made her way over to his table and sat down. "Hi, I'm Sandra Acaña. I'm glad you decided to meet with me about helping me with my campaign."

"I'm happy to. Tell me, why do you want to run for County Commissioner?"

"Well, I really want to make a difference in this community. I got my MFA here at the university, which I know doesn't sound very promising for a political candidate, but I have been working in retail for years now."

"Yes, because of your mother's business."

Sandra was taken aback that he knew that and said, "Yes, because of my mother's business, but also my own store in the mall."

"What did you study: fiction or poetry?"

"I am a poet."

"Well, poetry and politics come from the same place and in many ancient cultures, poets held esteemed politic positions."

"I didn't know that," she chuckled sounding like her mother.

Alejandro smiled, seeing so much of Melly in her. "Go on, tell me about your plans for being County Commissioner."

"I want to help the local business community. I want to make sure they are protected, and they have access to all of the protections of the major corporate stores."

"That's admirable but what about your constituents?"

"I want to help them too, but that's where I need help. My mother was much better at that than me."

"Your mom is such a strong woman and she certainly has the charisma to run for office. I wonder if you do as well."

"Yes, my mom did…but I don't want to talk about her. I want to talk about me," Sandra said starting to get a little upset.

"I'm sorry you are right. Let's talk about you," Alejandro sensed that she didn't like it when he brought up her mother.

"I really want this, and I am willing to do everything I can to win this. Anything," she said looking straight into his eyes with such determination that it scared him.

"Sandra, what do you mean anything?"

"I know you worked on the Betty Lynch campaign, and I heard it through the grapevine what you did for her, and I want you to know that I am willing to do the same," she said as she ran her hand down her blouse to her cleavage.

Alejandro was a bit insulted by this turn of events. Especially since no one knew about what happened between Betty and him. No one. "Sandra, I don't know what you have heard about me, but I am not like that."

"Are you sure because, like I said, I am willing to do anything," Sandra said even more determined.

Alejandro did not like where this was going at all especially since he had developed feelings for her mother and was hoping she would be here today with her daughter. "Sandra, if you really want me to work on your campaign then you have to stop that. You have to be a strong woman and never use your sexuality as a way to get ahead. This isn't the 80s anymore. This is 2006. Be the strong Chicana feminist that I saw in your thesis."

Sandra relaxed and put her hand down, "You read my thesis?"

"Yes, I did. You think I would come to a meeting without doing my research first."

"Good," Sandra said smiling, "I just wanted to make sure because so far that has been the luck I have had with managers."

Alejandro realized it was a test and now liked her even more. "Now, I can't actively work on your campaign and work at the university at the same time. I would have to take a leave of absence in order to be your manager, which I can't do right now, but I can still help you."

"How?"

"I can advise. Besides, I have someone better to be your manager."

"Who?"

"Your mother."

"My mother? Is that a joke? I don't think it's funny."

Alejandro, confused by this response, said, "Your mother has all of the qualities you would need in a good manager, and she really wants you to get this position."

Sandra narrowed her eyes in anger and said, "I know that's what she wanted. That's why I'm running, but she can't manage anything from where she is at. You asshole, I thought you did your research."

Baffled Alejandro asked, "What do you mean? Where is she?"

"She's been dead for over eight months now. She went to Matamoros one day, and she didn't come back."

Feeling like he was insane, he said, "That's impossible. I was just with her two days ago. She set this meeting up."

"I set this meeting up. She was always talking about you when she took your class two years ago. She couldn't stop going on and on about how great you were, but now I don't know what to think."

"But…"

Sandra got up and left in such a fury that Alejandro couldn't process what just occurred. He waited there for ten minutes before rushing back to his office and looking up Melly Palacios and finding out that she indeed had been dead for eight months. Alejandro looked around his office and saw the papers and books all over the floor, still left undisturbed from the night they had made love on his desk. As he was scanning the papers and books. He came upon the reports that Melly had left for him, and he picked them up. They were not reports on the Betty Lynch election but were news reports of Melida Palacios' disappearance.

knock. knock. knock.

Alejandro looked up and saw Melly Palacios standing there in the same clothes she had on the day he had met her, with the same books and papers in her hand.

"Dr. Leyva, can I speak with you?"

Alejandro just gaped at her and then said, "Sure, come on in."

She walked in and placed her books and papers down on his large oak desk. The desk itself was covered in papers and books, so she had to place her heavy books down on top of his. "I don't know if you remember me," he didn't, "I was in your Argument & Persuasion class last spring. My name is Melly Palacios, but I was Acaña back then. I am divorced."

THE ROAD TO LLORONA PARK

"Have you ever found yourself counting Mexicans?"

"What?"

"You know, you go into a restaurant, and you look around to see how many Mexicans there are besides you."

"I guess so, but how do you know they're all Mexicans, what if they are Cuban or Puerto Rican or something."

"Really, that doesn't even matter. We live on the border with Mexico, you're Mexican, I'm Mexican. Chances are they are going to be Mexican."

"True but I don't think we should make that assumption just because they are Latino."

"Don't even go there with that Latino bullshit, besides you are missing the point of my whole story."

"What story?"

"The one I was just telling you about counting Mexica… haven't you been listening?"

"Yes, I've been listening, but I didn't know you were telling a story, I thought you were asking a question."

"Whatever, you know the question was rhetorical."

"No, it wasn't."

"What, yes it was, I am the one who said it."

"Yes, but that is not what a rhetorical question is."

"Don't even lecture me on grammar when you just ended your sentence with a preposition, puto."

"Hey, don't get all defensive now. You are the one who is a woman now."

"True that, but you are still a puto."

This was the first time we had talked like friends since we left the Rio Grande Valley for Albuquerque, New Mexico. I had agreed to help my friend, Rolando now Rowena move from the Valley to Albuquerque because he/she, still not used to that, had gotten a job there. At least that is what Rowena has been telling me, but I know for a fact that it is more than that. We left McAllen around 6 in the morning, and it was somewhere outside of San Antonio, literally four hours into the trip before we began to speak to each other. The only interaction we had was: "Can you stop because I got to pee" or small talk about the changing towns of South Texas. I turned to Rowena and for the first time this entire trip, I really looked at her, with those black plastic teardrop shaped glasses and her long black curly hair. Piercing green eyes and thin cheekbones. There was nothing of Rolando in that face. She looked feminine. Content. Almost at peace with herself. She smiled and looked back at me.

"What? You never seen a post-op tranny before?" Rowena said with a bit of sarcastic bite in her words.

"No, actually I haven't. But I was just thinking that I don't see you anymore."

"What do you mean? I am right here."

"No, I mean I don't see Rolly anymore. He's gone. Isn't he?"

Rowena pushed her slowly sliding glasses up the brim of her nose and said, "Oh honey, Rolly never existed."

"Rolly existed. I knew him. We played soccer together as kids. We hung out and smoked pot together. We talked about writing and girls and getting out the Valley. Rolly was my friend. He existed," I don't know why I was so angry at Rowena for saying that, but I was.

"Hal, there is something that you have to realize. Rolly might have been real to you but to me, he was a character I slipped into every day. Like a costume."

"Pretty convincing costume."

"Hal, look at me for one second."

So, I did. I turned my eyes from an empty curving road and looked at her. She looked at me with wet green eyes and said, "It's still me. Maybe not with testicles and a dick or facial hair, but it's still me. The friend you grew up with is still me, but for the first time I am free of that Rolly costume. Does that make sense?"

I looked back at the road and watched the green road signs whizz by us. I watched as the road curved and never seemed to end. I stayed quiet for what seemed like hours but was only really seconds. "Look, Rowena," I finally said, "I'm not some homophobic asshole. I support what you did. I even understand it, but at the same time…"

"…your heteronormative masculine self can't accept it. Right?"

"I don't want that to be true."

"Listen, Hal, I get it. You are a liberal at heart but here's the thing. You only believe those things in theory. When you are face to face with it. That is when things get real, and most people can't handle it. But Hal, this is who I have always been. That is what you have to understand."

I looked back at her, and she smiled at me, and I felt a tension leave my body. I relaxed a little and gripped the steering wheel a little softer. Our first stop was Junction, TX. We had planned to stop, fuel up, grab something to eat, and head north through Lubbock to cut across to New Mexico, but Rowena had other plans.

Junction

So we stopped at this convenience store/BBQ joint with crazy animal sculptures in a fake grass covered patio. It had white metal patio furniture of all shapes and sizes. Inside was where you got your food. You could order from one to five meats and some sides to make it seems like you are balancing out your meal. There was a young Mexican boy with a thick West Texas accent cutting the meat and serving. His name was Manny, or at least that is what the white guy with the camouflaged cap at the register called him. We stopped and got some brisket plates and sat down inside on these wooden picnic tables painted white and red: the colors of Texas Tech University. There were two other tables that were filled with an older white couple and a middle-aged Latino looking couple. On the last table by this display of past Heisman Trophy winners was a table of young men who looked like college students. They all wore UT Longhorn T-shirts and blue jeans. I noticed them because they kept stealing glances at Rowena.

Rowena was wearing a loose-fitting Texas A&M T-shirt she got at orientation. Rowena had been an Aggie as a graduate student and when she got her PhD she only kept the T-shirts and the diploma as a reminder of her Aggie experience. I know it wasn't a pleasant time for her, and she told me that her grad school experience put a real strain on her marriage. However, I didn't think it was the A&M shirt that kept drawing their glances. Rowena was tall and thin and it she wore tight jeans that accentuated her luscious hormone-induced ass. Her breasts were not large, but they were ample, and because the shirt she was wearing was old, anyone could easily see through the armhole and catch a glance at her bright blue bra underneath.

I didn't know if she noticed it or not but to me it was very distracting and I didn't know why. I mean Rowena was an attractive woman but in my mind I couldn't let go of Rolly.

"Hey Rowena, I think those guys over there are checking you out," I whispered to her.

Rowena's eyes got really big, and she looked back at the

table with the college guys. They all smiled at her and she smiled back. "They're kind of cute, don't you think?"

"That really ain't my department."

"You straight guys and your fear of sounding gay. You can't admit if a guy is cute. Women find other women attractive, and we don't automatically think they're lesbians," Rowena said as she looked back from the college guys.

"That's not it. It is not some homophobic thing. I just don't think about guys that way. Never have." I didn't know if that was true but it sounded true and really couldn't think of a guy I wanted to see naked.

"You're thinking about it now, aren't you?"

"What? No. I'm not." But I was. She had tricked me into picturing half-naked guys and dicks. I quickly switched to thinking about naked women, but then something peculiar happened; I thought of Rowena and looked right at her and said, "I think we should go."

"What, why? I wanted to see if I could flirt with those guys."

"No, let's go. We got like ten hours to go before we even get out of Texas. Another four before we get to Albuquerque. I want to get on the road."

"Fifteen hours."

"What?"

"Fifteen hours to get out of Texas."

"No, that's not right, if we go up through…"

"I want to go through Las Cruces."

"Las Cruces? Why? That's way out of the way."

"This is my trip, my dime. I want to go through Las Cruces."

"Why Las Cruces?"

"Do you remember when we were kids, and your aunt used to tell us the story about La Llorona?"

"Yeah, so?" I had no idea where this was going, but she seemed serious, so I played along.

"Well, there is a Llorona Park in Las Cruces, and I want to see it."

"There's a Llorona Park in Las Cruces?" My interest was peaked, maybe for curiosity's sake rather than anything else.

"Yes, and the first time I found out about it was right before my surgery. There was this nurse that said she was originally from New Mexico and that every year they would go to Llorona Park on February 15th for a celebration."

"They would celebrate La Llorona?"

"She said it was like a Dia de los Muertos type of thing. They would leave stuff like baby food and pacifiers and baby blankets. Stuff like that. It was sort of like that virgin to appease the angry god."

"And you want to see it? But it's August."

Rowena leaned in and touched my hand gently, "I almost went. I mean I made it as far as El Paso but then I chickened out. I couldn't do it. I guess I was too nervous because of my surgery. But then I realized it wasn't nervousness. It was because I was going there in the body of a man and I needed to go there as a woman."

We were on the road down I-10 after her speech. We had decided to stop off in El Paso for the night, which gave us only six more hours of driving left to do. Luckily Rowena said she would do it. And that lasted for about two hours before she told me she was tired and wanted to take a nap. So, there I was behind the wheel again driving through miles and miles of nothing, except mountains and desert. There is something about desert nothingness that has both a calming serene feeling and a feeling of absolute solitude.

"Where are we?" Rowena said as she woke.

"Somewhere outside of Fort Stockton, I think."

"Sorry about flaking on the driving, never been good at long distance driving."

"That's alright; I drive a lot. Sometimes it seems like the road is my home, like Neal Cassady."

Rowena laughed and said, "You wish you were Neal Cassady. You're at best Ken Kesey."

"What? I'm not even Kerouac."

Rowena rolled her eyes at me and said, "Son, please. When was the last time you wrote anything?"

"What does that have to do with anything?"

"Kerouac was a writer. He wrote all the time. You…you haven't written anything in years."

I was hurt by this, "I write all the time for the paper and magazines."

"That don't count, and you know it."

"Fine, I don't know when the last time I wrote was. I guess I have been going through a dry spell."

"Dry spell my ass. I think it's your wife."

"You leave her out of this, and besides, she left me."

"That's what I mean. When was the last time you got laid?"

"I don't have to tell you that."

"Really, that long, huh?"

I stayed quiet for a while. I didn't want to think about the fact that the last time I had sex with someone other than myself was at least a year ago, and that was with Gina, my ex. I had messed that marriage up, and now I am living in my grandfather's house. I believe Rowena realized she had hit a sore spot because she said, "Hal, I'm sorry. I didn't mean to say that. It's been a long time for me too. In fact, I have never had sex as a woman. I'm a virgin."

"Really, how does that work?"

"Surgery gave me a clean slate."

"Do you have a hymen?"

"No, douche, but it's all unpenetrated down there."

This was the first time we had talked about anything remotely close to her transformation and it didn't feel as awkward as I thought it would be.

"So, umm, how does it work? You know, now…that…you… have…"

"A vagina!" Rowena blurted out so loudly that it almost seemed to make the car shake.

"Yeah."

"It feels right but like a brand new car. I am taking very good care of it, douching and all. Probably overly attentive but it's new, you know."

"So, have you thought about sex?"

"Oh, look at you. Finally, we have come around to it."

"Come around to what?"

"Sex. Sex. Sex. Sex. The sex bomb. You have finally dropped it. It only took eight hours, but you finally dropped it. How does it feel?"

"Fuck you."

"Sure, honey, right here, right now. We would have to pull over for that."

"Ha. Ha. Very funny. You know that's not what I mean." I don't know what bothered me the most: that she knew I was thinking about sex or that she knew how difficult it was for me to broach the subject and that she was really enjoying it. It was such a Rolly thing to do. For one second I saw my old friend once again…but with boobs.

Rowena saw that I was really bothered by the subject, but instead of pulling back from the conversation she pushed even harder. "I've done a lot of research on the subject. So much that I think the NSA might have flagged me or something because I was watching Youtube clips and tranny porn, both pre and post-op. I was obsessed with sex as a woman before the surgery…"

"And now?" I interrupted to try and change the subject.

"Now," she seemed to turn very solemn and quiet for a second, it was kind of eerie, "now, it's different. Before, when I was married to Claire, especially that last year we had stopped having sex altogether. It had literally been six months since we last fucked. Then came the day I came out to her, I knew it was going to be tough, but I did it. I was in full drag, red dress and heels and everything and you know what?"

"What?"

"She didn't even flinch. She just sat there and looked so disinterested that I knew it was over, once and for all. But then, something extraordinary happened. She got up, hugged me, I could feel her tears streaming down her cheeks, and then she kissed me passionately. She told me that she had never been so attracted to me as she was that moment. We had sex right there on the kitchen floor. It was probably the best sex we ever had and then afterwards, she went back to the bedroom packed my stuff and told me to leave." Rowena was staring at the moving desert landscape, but I could hear her tears through her words.

"What about the kids?" I asked to snap her back to reality.

"I see them every other weekend. But they are still young. I don't think they really understand what is happening yet, but they started calling me M'apa because they watch Transparent."

"Are they even old even to watch that show? That show has a lot of sex."

"I forward those parts for them."

"Wait, wait. You showed it to them? Does Claire know?"

"No, I'm not crazy. I want to see my kids, but it helps them understand. I think."

I looked at Rowena who was scrolling through her emails on her phone and said, "It will get easier for them."

She nodded her head and then said, "Hey, let's stop in El Paso tonight. There's a poetry reading at the Percolator tonight and I want to read."

"You write poetry?"

"Yes, I dabble, besides it's an open mic so if I suck it won't be too bad," Rowena said while she typed on her phone. "And I signed you up too."

"Wait, what?"

El Paso

We got to El Paso around 5 pm and checked into the first hotel we saw that didn't look like a trucker or prostitute joint. It was a chain hotel, but I didn't care. Rowena made a stink about supporting local businesses, but every locally owned joint was either worse than a dive or extremely expensive, so there we were at the Motel 6. I sat in the cheaply made, nice looking chair jotting down a poem about the current immigrant crisis and I wasn't liking it. I just didn't feel it. Rowena had been in the shower for about forty-five minutes now, and I was getting impatient. It took me ten minutes to shower and get dressed, but I guess since she is a woman now, she has inherited the long shower of a woman. I went back to the poem, scratched out lines and rearranged others, but nothing worked. So I did the only thing that felt right, I crumbled it up and wrote something new. And just as I finished it, the door to the bathroom opened and out came Rowena in a tight-fitting black dress with two solid blue stripes along her sides. It was the hem stopped far from her knees, which accentuated her long legs and the rockin' black stilettos worked to tighten her calves and thighs and forced her butt out. If I didn't know any better, I would never have known that I was looking at what used to be a man. She was beautiful—no scratch that—she was hot. She had let her hair down, which worked well with the dress and the look. I felt seriously underdressed because I just had on my green cargo pants and short sleeve button up shirt.

"How do I look?" she said legitimately asking my opinion.

I couldn't lie so I told her the truth, "You're a hottie."

Her smile went wide across her face, and she turned back to the bathroom mirror to finish her makeup. She puckered up and put on a dark red lipstick.

We arrived late to the reading, first because we grabbed dinner and second because we had trouble finding parking in the downtown area. It seemed like they were really aggressively revitalizing their downtown area and so many of the roads and street side parking was under construction. It was 8:30 and the reading was just getting started, so Rowena was happy about that. She had been messaging back and forth with the organizer all night just to make sure she could read. It was strange because I had never known Rolly to be into poetry at all, but he did get a PhD in literature, so the interest was obviously there. But as Rowena, she seemed very eager to read her work, which I had not heard yet. I had asked on the ride to El Paso, but she was reluctant to share. I dropped the subject when she told me she had signed me up.

The organizer was a big guy, muscular and tattooed, (very threatening) and wearing a #Ayotzinapa43 T-shirt. He seemed like a nice guy as Rowena introduced us to each other.

"Hi, I'm Robert Quitero. Local poet and organizer here."

"Hi, I'm Haldon Cruces, writer and chauffeur for Rowena here."

He chuckled a little and then leaned in and said, "This is a coffeehouse, but we got some liquor and beer in the back if you guys want. Even a little mota too."

"Yes, definitely," I answered a little too eager. I didn't realize I wanted a drink as bad as I did. Robert led us to a back entrance by the bathrooms and into an alleyway where there were several people pouring drinks from Coke cans and bottles and a guy passing out bottles of Dos Equis. I went around as everyone introduced themselves and shook hands, but for the life of me, I didn't remember anybody's names. I just remembered Jesse because he was pouring the Jack and Cokes and I knew I wanted one of those for sure. Robert waited for me and Rowena to get a drink and then announced that the reading was starting in five minutes, so everybody had to make their way inside.

It had been an hour and a half and they still hadn't called my name, which was fine if they forgot about me, but I knew that I wasn't that lucky. I had three Jack and Cokes already, and I was feeling the relaxing feeling of a buzz, but at the same time I was little annoyed because Rowena had left me sitting amongst a group of eager poets and she had spent the last hour and a half flirting with Robert. I was just waiting for this reading to be over so we could go back to the hotel room and get some sleep, but it didn't seem like things were going to go down that way. I had spent many a nights waiting in the car as Rolly went off to screw some girl he just picked up at a bar. It seemed to be a habit that Rolly kept when he became Rowena, and I didn't feel like waiting in the car while she fucks this guy in our hotel room. Robert finally called Rowena up to the mic, and she read a poem called Lilac Mariposa about being a strong Chicana. It had some good imagery in it but lacked a sense of authenticity. When she finished, everyone clapped and cheered, and she looked me directly in the eyes and smiled. I smiled back and clapped for her too. She finally made her way to me as Robert called up another poet.

Rowena sat down next to me on the overly comfortable green coffeehouse couch. "So, what did you think?"

"It was good. I liked the metaphor about the caterpillar

sloughing off its old body and turning into a beautiful lilac butterfly."

"Are you being sarcastic? I really can't tell right now."

"No, I am not being sarcastic. It was good."

She didn't seem to completely buy it, but she let it go and said, "Robert's a sweet guy. Don't you think?"

"Yeah, he seems nice. Is he going to be the one to pop your tranny cherry?"

Rowena looked at me with fury in her eyes and said, "Is that what you think of me? That I'm just here to pick up some guy. You don't think I'm truly interested in poetry."

It was then that I realized it wasn't anger in her eyes, it was hurt. She really did value my opinion. "I'm sorry, Rowena. It's just that, you know, back in the day, you would pick up chicks and leave me to be the getaway driver."

"Did you just make a Steve McQueen El Paso reference?"

"Oh yeah, the Getaway, that was here right?"

"Don't change the subject but yeah."

"Sorry, I just felt...I don't know...he just seems too good of a guy and muscles and tattoos and..." I looked at her at this point and saw that she was smiling, "What?"

"Are you jealous?"

"Jealous? What? No."

Rowena laughed and said, "Oh my God, you are jealous of Roberto."

"No, no, that's not it. That is not it at all."

"You know the more you deny it, the more I know it's true. That's so sweet."

"Rowena, wait...no, no, no, I just want to...you know...I..."

Then it happened. I was saved by the one thing that I dreaded the most until this moment. Robert called my name, and I sprang up and walked up to the mic. I felt Rowena slap my ass as I walked away but I didn't react. I was too focused on the poem I was going to read. So I got up to the mic and looked out at the sea of eager poets, and then I saw Rowena with a big smile on her face. I pulled out the poem I wrote in the hotel room...

I will wait here 'til the wolves come back. I don't care if they eat me. take me
into the fold. There's gotta be an answer at the end.

I will uncover the plot of the black hat. it's scarier than anything
else. it hides secret truths about. who we really are. I will lift up the
brim and see. there's gotta be an answer at the end.

everything needs an end. we always see dawn. breaking of day.
cracking light on the edge of the horizon. we always see. but the end
we don't see. there's gotta be an answer at the end.

torture me like you torture them. we are all locked in like hope in
Pandora's box. squashed by darkness, despair, & pure unfiltered
Apathy. there's gotta be an answer at the end.

slowly unraveling things left raveled. Inside glass jar. almost invisible in right
light. voice in head saying stop. go no further. forget.
there's gotta be an answer at the end.

I read this poem at Rowena. I read it with locked eyes on the
hotel room stationery, but I read it to her. I didn't know what the
poem meant then, but I knew she did because when I looked up,
her eyes were holding back a river of emotions. No tears but a
wall of wetness glistening in the fluorescent lighting. I got off
the makeshift stage and everyone clapped after a few seconds of
silence. I walked over to her and sat down back in my spot. She
turned to me and said, "See, I knew there was a poet in there."

Before I could respond back, Robert called Rowena back up
to the stage and so, like a light getting flicked on, her eyes were
clear again and the masking smile was back. She sprung up and
walked back to the stage where she read a collaborative poem
with Robert and then at the end they shared a kiss, which made
me uncomfortable enough to turn my gaze from them. It wasn't
my heteronormativity that was offended; it was something else.

"Hey, I really liked your poem," a voice shook me from my
thoughts. I turned to see this cute dark-skinned Latina wearing
oversized glasses and a Chingona Power T-shirt.

"Thanks," I said, "it's not finished yet. It's a work in

progress."

"Aren't we all? My name is Natalie," she said with an outstretched hand. I took her hand and noticed she had a small tattoo of the Aztec calendar on her wrist.

"I'm Hal. I'm not from around here."

"Oh really, where are you from?" she said as she slid down next to me on the couch. We were too close for two people who just met, but the couch sagged in the middle, so it forced everyone to the center.

"I'm from the Rio Grande Valley," she didn't look like she knew where that was so I clarified, "down near South Padre Island."

That she recognized and so she said, "Okay, I went there for Spring Break once when I was an undergraduate."

"So you are a graduate student now?"

"Yeah, I'm studying Chicana literature. You?"

As we talked about our lives and I found out more and more about this poet and scholar, I realized that I was flirting in a way that I hadn't done since before I was married. I hadn't really thought about hooking up, but now with Natalie and her almost revealing low-cut T-shirt, things were certainly stirring down below. We talked for what seemed like an hour before we decided to go back to the alleyway and get a couple more drinks. Things were going well. She was laughing at all of my stupid jokes, and I was seriously digging her sexy Chicana feminist vibe. We even walked away from the crowd of poets and stood at the end of the alleyway for a little privacy. Things were going too well when I heard a voice interrupt our conversation.

"Hey, how's it going? I was looking everywhere for you." It was Rowena, and she didn't sound happy.

"Oh hey, Rowena, sorry I just got lost track of time. I've been talking with Natalie here."

Rowena looked at Natalie with eyes that if I didn't know any better, looked like jealous, territorial eyes. She said *hi* and Natalie responded like a woman who didn't know she was hitting on a married man. It was very strange. "Natalie here is a poet and Chicana scholar. You two should probably talk since that is right up your alley. Rowena here is going to head up the Chicano Studies Department at UNM."

"Hey," Rowena said. "Are you a first-year grad student?"

"Yes, how did you know?"

"I can tell by the T-shirt."

I was picking up some really weird vibes here, and Natalie kept looking back at me with a look like a trapped animal. "Yeah, it's all about brown girl power, right?"

"Yeah, hey, Natalie is it?" Rowena said to Natalie trying her best not to create any more awkward tension.

"Yes."

"Can I have a word with Hal here for just a second?"

"Yeah, sure, I just want to say I didn't know you two were together," Natalie said as she quickly made her exit back inside.

I tried to stop her, "Natalie, wait, we are not..." but it was too late, I had blown my chance or more accurately Rowena had blown my chance.

When she was inside, I turned to Rowena and said, "What the hell was that?"

"What do you mean? You mean little miss Anzaldúa groupie?"

"Yeah, I liked her."

"She's too young for you and besides it would never work. She'll marry some white guy and forget about you."

"Ouch. What is going on with you?"

"What do you mean?"

"Obviously, you are upset. What happened? Roberto turn you down?"

Rowena shot daggers at me with her stare and said, "You are such an asshole sometimes, you know."

"Me? You are the one who just cock-blocked me with your phantom cock."

"I didn't cock-block you; that's not how it works."

"Whatever." I was really upset, and I didn't know what was happening here.

"I wasn't going to fuck him if that's what you were thinking."

"Why not? He's also muscles and macho and shit."

Rowena stepped really close to my face and whispered, "He's F to M, you shithead. Pre-op."

It took me a second to decrypt that to mean that he was a female to male transsexual. "So no…you know."

"Yes, he doesn't have the equipment if that matters anyway. You are so straight sometimes; it drives me crazy."

Something had broken between us, and all we could do is stare at each other. I didn't know what to say to put this friendship back together, and I don't think Rowena did either, but there we were, right in the middle of a trip. We were stuck together for at least a whole other day.

"Hal, I want to go to Llorona Park."

The anger had passed in me, and I could tell by her tone that it had passed for her as well.

"Sure, we will go in the morning."

"No, we have to go now."

"Now, but that park is in Las Cruces." She didn't flinch so I continued, "in New Mexico." Again nothing. "That's like an hour away." Once again she was a statue.

Las Cruces

We rode in silence. The park was only about an hour away, but it felt like two. The entire time Rowena was typing away on her phone. Every time I tried to spark up a conversation, she shushed me. Like a child. Rowena was Zen focused on whatever she was typing. I really had no idea where I was going, so I let the GPS navigate the whole way. In the dark, the desert looks like nothing. No landscape. No lights. No horizon to let you know where the road ended and the sky began. All I could see was what the headlamps allowed. Twenty feet of lit asphalt. It was almost like I was driving on a bed of darkness until on the right I saw two headlights and the persistent sound of a train horn. At first I couldn't really tell where it was, it looked like it was heading right for us but then miraculously it ended up on our left and shot off into the night.

The only sound I had was the click-click-clicking of Rowena

typing away on her phone. After awhile that sound became music to my ears until Siri came on the car speakers and said, "Exit in half a mile."

"We're almost there."

Rowena finally looked up. She stopped typing and shoved her phone in the cleavage of her left breast. "Good," was all she said.

The park itself wasn't much to look at. It was a thin strip of land with a small playground and a few benches. It wasn't really lit up at night either. It had only one streetlamp and that mostly lit up the building and small parking lot and building at the end of the park. There was a chain link gate barring us from parking in the lot, so Rowena told me to just park on the shoulder of the road. In the dark, I really couldn't see the Rio Grande River that the park ironically cradled, but I could hear the wind moving the waves ever so gently.

Rowena turned on the flashlight app on her phone and we made our way down toward the bridge, which divided the park. After a few steps of walking in her stilettos she took them off and began to walk barefoot on the gravel and grass. I walked closely behind her until we reached the concrete sidewalk that led to the under-bridge. She stopped and said, "Do you remember when I said I had never been here before?"

"Yeah, that was earlier today."

"Well, I lied. I have been here before," she said with a deadpan voice devoid of emotion, "It was a long time ago when we were kids. We were in ROTC, remember?"

"Yeah, I was only in it one year, though," I said feeling worried about where this conversation was leading.

"I was in it all four years of high school. I loved it because it made me feel more like a man. Discipline. Guns. Tight uniforms. Well, maybe that is too homoerotic, but anyway. There was this time when we took a field trip to visit colleges and New Mexico State was one of them..."

"...yeah, I remember that trip. We were juniors and you were all decked out in your military dress."

"That's because Gunny Sargent Tamez was one of the

chaperones and there were a handful of us that were ROTC. Well, we came here that night," Rowena said turning toward the under-bridge and pointing the light inside. "This is where it happened."

I was confused. I didn't remember coming here at all. I only remembered the hotel and staying up all night talking to the girl I liked at the time. Her name was Suzie, and she was a cheerleader. She liked to read, but we never came to La Llorona Park. "I don't understand," I said, "what happened here?"

"Do you remember Gunny Sergeant Tamez? At the time, he must have just been in his thirties. You know a Grenada Vet. Chiseled and cute."

"I remember Gunny, but I don't remember any of that."

"Well, I had a crush on him. He was so…hot, and I was just a young kid, still struggling with my sexuality. Well, on the night that we got here and we stayed at that Motel 6, you were off with Suzie the cheerleader, you were so in the friend zone with her."

"Was not…"

"Hal, really, she had you wrapped around her finger, but anyway, this is my story. On that night, me and some of the guys were talking about La Llorona Park because we wanted to know if she would actually be there. We also wanted to buy some beer and get drunk. Well, Gunny overheard and instead of disciplining us, he agreed to buy us some beer and take us there. I had butterflies in my stomach because I knew he caught me looking at him and he knew before I did what I was. I was like a little girl with a crush around him, but you know as a guy. So, we went," and this is where Rowena walked under the bridge and I could tell something was wrong.

"Rowena, are you alright?"

She turned and looked at me and tears were streaming down her face. She quickly wiped them away and then pulled her phone from her cleavage and pulled up her something on her screen, "I wrote it down so I could get it right." She cleared her throat and continued her story. "You know, we were drinking and I wasn't much of a drinker back then. Even though I pretended I was, I really wasn't, but anyway. The other guys went over to the jungle gym and were messing around on the slide. You know, just messing around. Sergeant Tamez took me aside and we talked and talked about movies and the military and then he led me under this bridge. It was dark and we only had the moonlight. When we were where we are now, we sat down and listened to the river. Then it happened. It was subtle like hot breath on wet skin. He touched me. Gently on the arm. My hairs stood up and I felt the electric shock of anticipation creep up my arms and down my spine and down my crotch. He pulled me close. I turned to look into his eyes but everything was black and all I could make out was an outline. Then, his lips were so close to mine that I could smell the beer on his breath. I wanted the kiss. This was a dream come true, but then…but then…he said, "Is this what you want, faggot?" and then he grabbed my dick. I had a raging hard-on and I didn't even notice, I so wanted that kiss. He grabbed it so hard that I thought he was going to break it off. That is when I started to pull back but he was so strong."

Rowena stopped reading and wiped the tears off of her face that were colored with mascara giving her the look of a sad clown. It wasn't funny. It was just heartbreaking. I knew what she was going to say next, but I needed to hear it.

She continued, "He turned me over on my stomach. He had me pinned down. I couldn't move. I couldn't even breath, but somehow he pulled my pants down and I felt him. Inside me. It hurt so bad. I don't know if it was the physical pain or the pain of being violated that hurt most. It didn't take him long and afterwards he just pissed into the river and I just lay there trying not to cry. Then he said, "Get up, we have to get back. We have an early morning tomorrow." And he just walked off like nothing happened. I did what he said. I got up, pulled my pants up and limped back to the rest of the guys."

Rowena stopped there and put her phone down and looked down at the dark river. After about a minute of silence, she continued, not even looking at her phone, "I never told anybody what happened that night. Never. I didn't want to be gay anymore and so I went after every pretty girl I could and slept with as many as I could. I told myself that I was the one that was wrong.

I also never went back to ROTC after that either. I would always skip class, but the Sergeant passed me anyway. Then when we graduated high school, I left and never looked back. It took me a long time to come to terms with the fact that it wasn't my fault I got raped and even longer to admit that I was trans. You are the first person I have ever told, I never even told Claire and I don't ever plan on telling my kids."

I knew I needed to say something, so I said the first thing that came to mind, "Is that why you had to come here? To confront the demons of your past?"

"This is La Llorona Park; it is named after the stealer of children. It stole me, well my childhood."

"I'm sorry, Rowena, I wish there was…"

"…that's not the end of it. There's more. The real reason we are here. About five years ago, I was completing my PhD and I was home for Thanksgiving. My dad always kept up with the news. He is a news junkie and he kept every paper since 1965 in our garage. But anyway, he wanted to show me that one of my former teachers was retiring and the school was honoring him for his thirty years of service. The ceremony was on the upcoming Monday. He handed it to me and there it was, Gunnery Sergeant Ernesto Tamez. He looked the same except he had grey hair now and a few wrinkles. He was smiling and that just set me off. Hal, you have to understand that I didn't even remember doing any of this, but I decided to go to the ceremony. I took my father's pistol, the one he always thought he hid from us in his closet. I made sure it was loaded and I stuck it in the small of my back like I saw in the movies. And I went. It was like I was in a daze, some sort of trance. I was going to kill him. I got there and I saw him standing there in his dress blues, greeting past students and parents. I reached back to make sure the gun was there and it was. I didn't have a plan. I was just going to shoot him. I got in line with the rest of them. And I waited. And then… and then…the most amazing thing happened…A kid came up to him, out of nowhere and threw red paint all over him. He screamed, "Rapist. Molester. You are a monster." It was then that I snapped out of my trance. I was able to realize something.

I looked at that kid and I saw all of his pain and I saw myself. And I realized that killing him wouldn't have done anything but destroy me. I turned around and left. I heard they covered up the incident and Sergeant Tamez was arrested and convicted and is now in prison. But that is beside the point. It was that moment when I let it all go. I forgave myself for what happened and it was then that I decided that I wasn't going to lie about who I was anymore. That was the day I chose to become a woman."

"Jesus, Roll—Rowena, I never knew. I mean I remember that story about a ROTC instructor getting arrested for an inappropriate relationship with a student but I never knew," I reached over and hugged her. She hugged me back and collapsed into sobs against my shoulder. She tried to speak but the cries drowned out her words.

After a few minutes of a good cry she wiped her tears on my shirt and said, "But I'm not finished."

I was confused. I didn't know what else she could say.

"The reason you are here. You had to have wondered why I asked you."

"Well, yes, but I just thought since we were friends for so long that…"

"…that is part of the reason, but I have an ulterior motive."

I didn't know what she was going to say, but I was already beginning to feel uncomfortable.

"I asked you to take this trip with me and here because I have always loved you, Hal. You have been my one true friend through childhood, high school, college, and even though we haven't spoken in a few years, I knew you would do this."

"I love you too. We're friends. Always will be." I didn't know where this was going, talking about love, but I knew it wasn't going to end well for me.

"Hal, I brought you here because this is the place where I lost my innocence as a man. It was my first time with anybody and it was so brutal and cruel and so devoid of any love…" she paused her for a few seconds and looked me in the eyes and I knew what she wanted but I needed her to say it. She said, "I want my first time as a woman to be with someone I love. I want it to be you."

And there it was. I guess I knew all along that this is where this whole thing was heading but I didn't want to believe it. I broke her gaze and stood up. Every fiber of my being wanted me to run as far from this situation as possible. This was insane. This was Rolly and yet, she is Rowena.

"Hal? Can you say something please?" her voice sounded shaky.

I turned back to look at her. The light from her phone spotlighted her face perfectly. I don't know if she planned that or not but in that face I couldn't see my friend, Rolly. All I could see was Rowena. "Rowena, I don't know. I mean I want to be there for you but what you are asking is…is…I don't know."

"It's a little out of your comfort zone."

"A little? A little? This is so far out of my comfort zone that I don't even know what to feel or say or anything. Why me? I mean, why not some hot guy at a bar?"

"I don't want it to be some frivolous fling. I want it to mean something."

"Rowena, I don't know."

Rowena smiled for the first time since we got to the park and she said, "That's not a no."

I didn't realize that I had never said no either, but I wanted to say no, but why couldn't I? What was stopping me from just shutting down this whole invitation? Was it because she is my friend and I don't want to hurt her or is it…no, I can't think that.

"Rowena, let's just go back to El Paso and we can discuss it later. I need time."

She stood up and simply said, "Okay. I understand." Her response was cold, almost robotic.

Back in El Paso

We rode the entire way back in silence. I think that we were both so lost in our own thoughts that we didn't even feel the hour go by. We got back to the hotel room and she went to the bathroom mirror and just stood there looking at herself. I was by the door looking at her look at herself and for the first time I realized something. This was not Rolly. It never was. This is Rowena. She is she. And so I walked up to her. Stood right behind her and I broke her trance. She looked at me through the mirror. I touched her shoulder and she turned around. Our eyes locked and I said, "Hello, Rowena."

"Hello, Haldon."

And I kissed her and she kissed me back.

Albuquerque

We made it to Albuquerque late the next afternoon. It was only a four hour drive but we slept in late and took our time leaving the hotel room. The trip to her new place was pretty uneventful. Rowena had found a duplex unit that wasn't too far from the university. It was already pre-furnished so she didn't need to really bring much but her books and clothes. We had somehow loaded four suitcases into the backseat of the car and four more in the trunk, leaving my duffel bag to find a home in the floorboards under the driver's seat. I unloaded her stuff by myself because she was too busy on her phone working out details about department meetings and scheduling. She was set to start classes in a week and she didn't have much time to settle in. I only stayed in Albuquerque for two days. Rowena had booked me a flight back home since it was her car that we had ridden in. We did go up and down Route 66 and visited the Nob Hill area around the university. It was a good two days and I really didn't want to leave.

My time there in Albuquerque was like a vacation from my life. From everything that I thought that I was. We just spent time together. Friends. And sometimes it felt like we were a couple. I chose not to think about my heteronormative hang-ups as Rowena calls it and then I just was. It was the best time I had since my divorce. We never really talked about what happened at Llorona Park the entire time I was there. We did talk about staying in communication through telegram. Rowena thought it would be great to free ourselves from modern technology and so I agreed to send her a telegram when I got home. At the airport, we did share a parting kiss packed with everything that goes with it. The not wanting the kiss to end, the desire to stay, the pain of leaving, of longing to see her again. It was what it was.

THE SUBLIME DRESS

Stephen Reyna was an ugly man. An ugly man in an ugly suit. He lived an abnormally ordinary life and lived in an abnormally ordinary apartment. He had nothing in his life that was of any importance, not to anyone whom he knew or even himself, except for one thing. A red dress. It hung on a hook on his wall in his bedroom, positioned perfectly so that every time he got up from his ugly old bed he would see it. The red dress. It was a short dress with nothing exceptional about it, except that it was beautiful. In cut. In style. And in its plainness. It was beautiful in a way that made the room unordinary and that made Stephen feel less ugly. He had never worn this red dress; he simply looked at it every day before he went to bed and when he woke up. It was the only beautiful thing in his life and the only thing he desired in his life was looking at this red dress.

He had often thought about wearing it, this vestido rojo as he called it. He had thought about putting this dress on with that new pair of black pumps that were stored on the shelf in his closet, but he never did. He never had the courage. He just looked at it and dreamed of what this dress would be like if it could be worn. Would it make him beautiful? Would it turn him from the ugly man in the ugly suit that lived in an abnormally ordinary life into something better? Would the beauty of this dress make his life sublime? He liked the word, sublime. He liked the way it sounded. It reminded him of putting a lime in a 7 UP and it tasting better than anything that he ever tasted before in his life. Sublime. It meant something so beautiful it could only be celestial. So beautiful it was terrifying. He liked that. To be so beautiful that the only emotion it triggers is terror. Imagine that, he thought, to have that kind of effect. But he knew he never could because he was an ugly man and he owned only 3 brown suits. One that was his father's before he died. One that he bought when he went for his first job interview 20 years ago. And one he bought 5 years ago so that he wouldn't have to do laundry all the time. It took him 15 years to buy a new suit and make a change because change did not come easyly to Stephen.

Change was a scary thing. It meant that the ordered world he had known would no longer exist and then what would he do? But change intrigued him because he saw the world around him change with such ease and he didn't know how it did it. Everyone else must be so comfortable in their own skin that change is just as simple as walking out the door every morning. But even that was a chore for Stephen because leaving his apartment was always the hardest thing for him to do. He worked as a manager for a data entry company at the Trade Zone, exactly 1 mile from the Mexican border. He managed 4 full-time employees and several part-timers. He worked the graveyard shift from 11 pm to 7 am Sunday through Thursday. It made him into a night owl, sleeping in the day and being up all night. He didn't watch too much TV because he didn't have cable and the late night shows were filled with beautiful people with extraordinary lives, and he was so ugly and normal. It was the opposite of sublime.

He didn't know the word for that. Maybe there wasn't one because no one but him ever felt that way, so he decided to create his own word. It took him many years to come up with a word because he was not very creative. Not with words. Not with anything really. He tried taking the word apart and separating it into two words—sub and lime—sub meant below so the opposite of below is above, so maybe top—and the opposite of lime is something sweet like a kiwi—but topkiwi didn't make any sense, so he tried kiwitop and that didn't work—so he tried different variations like sky and roof and ceiling but no word would work, and lime was fruit, so it didn't really have an opposite, so he tried colors—limes were green, so the opposite of green which is bright is black but then he thought every colors opposite was black—then it came to him, something simple—black—that was the word he came up with. That described what he felt. It was the opposite of everything. It wasn't very creative, but then Stephen wasn't creative. He never was.

The night was black, and that was his world. He only shopped at all-night pharmacies and only ate at all-night restaurants when no one was likely to be there. 4 AM. That was his time to go out and be in the world. That was when all of the late-night party kids were off the road, home, or in hotel rooms having sex. And those who rose early were not quite out in the world. Night. The blackest time of day was his time. It was his feeling. It was him. Except...

...he had that red dress, hanging on a hook on his bedroom wall. A little piece of beauty in his black world. It was the only thing out of place in his life. And for some reason, he couldn't imagine his life without it.

Stephen lived on the second story of an apartment complex that was mostly rented out to people who lived on welfare. Stephen was not on welfare. He lived simple and made decent money being a data entry manager. The reason Stephen lived here is because he had lived here since he was 18 years old and he got his first job doing date entry at the Trade Zone, graveyard shift of course. He rented the apartment when it was newly built about 20 years ago, and it wasn't welfare housing then. It had only become welfare housing about 10 years ago and Stephen's neighbors changed from working class Joe's with decent cars to single mothers with three children who don't work or severely underemployed mechanics with always 3 or 4 broken down cars in the parking lot. It seemed that no one here ever really left their apartments. Stephen had thought about leaving because, on most weekends the tenants of the Silver Street Apartment complex would party all-night in the decrepit family areas of the complex blaring their mixture of hip hop, rancheros, and Tejano music. The walls were thin in this building. He could hear everything. Stephen couldn't move, though he was comfortable. And the landlord didn't want to kick him out because he was one of the only tenants that actually paid him on time and never complained about anything going wrong in the apartment. Stephen was quiet and considerate and usually only exchanged a few words with the other tenants. Mostly in Spanish. Stephen spoke English, Spanish, and Tex-Mex fluently and he was a good speller too.

Spelling was one of the only things that Stephen could do well. In school he was spelling bee champion for 3 years running, and he had the trophies in his closet to prove it. For every competition that he won, he received a set of really nice leather bound Oxford English Dictionaries. These were the only books on his shelf. He would go back to them every day and pick out ten random words and write them down on a legal pad he kept on his tiny dining room table. He had been doing this for years and so far he had accumulated over 1000 legal pads. He often repeated words in his pads because he needed to remember how they were spelled. He even had the Spanish Dictionary, which he would buy yearly and do the same thing with Spanish words. Spelling properly in both languages was important to Stephen. Maybe because it was what made him good at his job. When he was a simple data entry clerk, he always maintained a 0% mistake rate in his entries, which was unheard of by company standards. Words were important to Stephen even if he didn't really understand what they all meant. They were important. Just like the red dress. He often thought about the words, 'red' and 'dress' and what they meant. He wanted to create a great story about the red dress but he couldn't. He wasn't creative enough. So he stole the story of the dress from his neighbor, Sheila.

Sheila was an abandoned single mother raising 4 children on her own. Each of the children were each born a year and a month apart almost exactly. Stephen liked that about her because it was consistent and Stephen loved consistent. Sheila was the closest thing to a friend that he had. She was 5 foot 9 inches tall, which was very tall for a Mexicana. She was light-skinned with dyed red hair and fake green eyes. Stephen knew they were fake because he had seen her when she had black eyes, but that was rare. She worked at a local bar as a waitress, but never reported it because if she did, she would lose her benefits from the state. She always told Stephen that the money they gave her wasn't enough for 4 kids, and she never had any help from their sperm donor of a father. She spoke English well enough, but the Spanish accent would creep in when she wasn't paying attention.

Sheila was a night owl. She was a wannabe writer and the only time she had to write was late at night when she got home from work and the children were all asleep. During the day she slept a lot because her children were all in school. Her children were each 12, 11, 10, and 9 respectively. She had all of her children when she was 15, 16, 17, and 18 and for twelve years she has worked as a waitress at one restaurant, bar, or anything that would take her with a GRE and inflexible time schedule. She wasn't a dumb girl; she was actually quite intelligent. In school, she had always tested very well and even made the honor roll several years in a row. But she was always taller than the boys and that made her very self-conscious. Boys were always intimidated by her height and that coupled with the fact that she was a late bloomer didn't help her self-esteem at all. Sheila was always creative and a loner in high school until one day Johnny Mata paid attention to her. She was 14 years old. He asked her out and she was overjoyed, so much so that when he started to touch her and run his hands up her skirt she didn't resist. Even when he pulled her panties down and took her virginity, she didn't resist. She was sure that this was the only way she was going to get a boy. Luckily for her it was enjoyable. Not at first, but afterwards. Then they were having sex every time they got together, until the moment she found out she was pregnant.

Sheila's parents weren't exactly parents per say. They were sperm and egg donors because they were also young parents who got pregnant in high school. Sheila was the first of three children. Her mother was also fifteen when she first got pregnant. She had been with the same boy until he became a man and then that man who Sheila never really knew, left her mother when she was four, after the birth of her little brother, and she never saw him again. Just about the same time, her mother checked out as well, leaving her children with Sheila's grandparents, and they were the ones who raised her from that point on.

When Sheila told her grandmother, she just sighed and said, "Aye, mijita! Not you!" Sheila's grandfather didn't say anything to her; he just got in his pick-up with his shotgun and went over to Johnny's house, picked him up and took them both to Mexico for a quick ceremony. That was how they got married. Literally a shotgun marriage. Johnny cheated on her every chance he got, which was fine with Sheila's grandfather as long as he worked and supported Sheila. Which he did, working at a mechanic shop with his brother and cousin. Sheila was forced to drop out of school after her first child, and she was made into a housewife. Her grandmother taught her how to cook, clean, and take care of children. Sheila did everything her grandmother said, but in her heart she was disappointed she never got to finish school. She loved school. She loved learning and stories. Being a housewife was boring to Sheila, so she bought several notebooks and checked out a lot of books from the library. She wrote every chance she got and read instead of watching telenovelas like her grandmother. That was her only mental escape.

Johnny became mean and drunk all of the time. He never really hit her, but he made her do things sexually that Sheila was never comfortable with and she never really loved him, so she treated him just as badly through other means. Mostly through intentionally mismanaging his money and hiding his beer so he would go out and get more. It would usually take him a few hours to come home. Sheila loved that. It was a horrible marriage from the start and when he left after their 4th child. Sheila was happy but at the same time devastated because she now had to work and she had no experience, so she took up waitressing and has been that ever since. But she could only take under the table jobs because she was on welfare and if they found out they would take away her benefits. She did get government housing after Johnny left and that is how she ended up at the apartments on Silver Street. Her grandmother would take care of the kids when she was at work and she would stay up all night writing and reading.

Another aspect of Sheila's life changed when Johnny left; she finally saw herself as a beautiful woman and started to enjoy her new role as a single woman. Going out on Friday and Saturday nights and spending plenty of nights in the back of cars or in hotel rooms with a different guy every time. This was something she never had when she was married to Johnny: a sex life, a chance to choose for herself. She was awakened sexually, but none of the guys that hit on her were ever that interesting. They only wanted one thing, and that was not a steady relationship with a mother of 4. Then one night after a bad sexual experience, drunk and stumbling, she went to the wrong apartment door and found her key didn't work. It was about five minutes of messing with the keys that the door flung open, and there was Stephen looking perplexed.

Sheila looked right up at him. He was an average looking guy with a plain white t-shirt and grey pajama shorts with night slippers on. She knew him as the weird guy next door who wore suits in the Valley, which was rare because it was usually too hot to wear a suit. She looked directly at him and said, "Sorry, wrong apartment."

"Yes, you are in 2D, this is 3D," Stephen said as he was closing the door.

"Wait," Sheila didn't know why she wanted to strike up a conversation with him, but she did. Maybe she was starved for conversation and he was just weird enough to be interesting. "What's your name?"

"Stephen Reyna."

"I'm Sheila."

"Hello," Stephen didn't know where this was going.

"Hey, do you mind if I come in? My kids are asleep and I don't want to disturb them."

Stephen just stood there contemplating what she was doing. He said nothing.

Sheila knew this was strange, so she said, "I want to sober up a little before I go home. I don't want to stumble around knocking stuff over and wake my kids."

Stephen opened the door, he didn't know why. Maybe because her breasts were almost spilling out of her dress, maybe because he wanted someone to talk to as well. He never knew why he let her in, but he did.

"Do you want some coffee?"

"Sure," she said as she walked in and plopped herself down on his aged couch. The TV was on and a movie was paused. She didn't recognize the still on the screen, so she asked "What are you watching?"

"It's a documentary on spelling bees."

"You like spelling bees."

"I was a championship speller."

"Great. I am a writer."

And that was what started their friendship. With a conversation. That night they had sex. Stephen couldn't understand why a beautiful woman like Sheila would sleep with him but she did, and it wasn't the only time. Their relationship was more about conversation than anything else. Stephen figured that she only slept with him because she was horny and not because she was attracted to him. When they did have sex, it was in his bedroom, and he knew she saw the red dress but never said anything about it. Never even acknowledged it was there. Stephen began to question if it really existed at all, so he began touching the dress every day to make sure it was real.

Then one day after they had sex, Stephen finally asked, "Why don't you ever ask me about the red dress on the wall?"

"I figured you'd tell me when you felt like it."

"I don't know why I have it."

"Was it your wife's or something?"

"No, I've never been married."

"Then whose is it?"

"It's mine, and I have a pair of pumps to match in the closet as well."

"Great, at least you have fashion sense. Shoes are usually the most important part of an outfit."

Stephen was astonished. She didn't care that he had a dress with shoes. She didn't even seem shocked or even disgusted. He was an ugly man, and someone ugly shouldn't have beauty in his life, but he did. The dress and now Sheila, but he knew Sheila wouldn't last. The dress would.

"So what's the story, morning glory?" Sheila asked as she got up and walked over to the dress and ran her fingers over it.

Stephen looked at her, comfortable in her nakedness, standing next to the dress and when she touched it, the dress became more beautiful. Maybe it was for her. Maybe the dress was meant for someone beautiful and not for someone ugly like him.

"It's beautiful," he said, "like you. Sublime."

"Sublime. I don't think I'm sublime. I'm not that beautiful."

"Sure you are."

"Do you have a story for this dress?" Sheila asked him.

"No. I don't. I'm not that creative."

"Then I will make one up for you."

Stephen was flabbergasted. He needed a story and here was one going to be presented to him. Stephen stood up and walked over to her and hugged her and cried. He had never cried before and never in front of anyone. He didn't know what he was feeling, but it wasn't ugly. It was something else. Sheila held him tight and cried herself, but she didn't know why. They stood there, two naked bodies embracing each other.

Sheila spoke first. "The story of the dress is simply this. It doesn't have a story. It has always been here. On the wall. Hanging in a plain room with a man who thinks he's ugly. This dress, he believes, is the only beauty in his life and that makes this dress sublime because its beauty shakes him to his very core. It unnerves him. Making him feel just a little less ugly. This dress is not real. Just like the shoes in his closet to match. They don't really exist because beauty doesn't really exist. Beauty only exists because we say it does. This dress. This sublime dress only exists because you have created it."

Stephen looked up at her face, which had tears streaming down and couldn't say a word because that was the story.

STRANGE LEAVES

#immigrationshuffle

Steps off of bus. Downtown McAllen. After surrendering to Border Patrol. Given ticket to see judge in 3-6 months. Options are simple: take bus ride to detention center deep in U.S. territory or report to refugee center located 2 blocks south of bus station. Shī barely understands since only knows few words English and not much more Spanish. Shī mostly spoke Quechua. Shī mostly gestures and points on Border Patrol paper map. Shī points at church. Symbol she knows well. cruz blanco…white cross…salvation she hopes. Shī walks down city block filled with tiendas, parking garages, and loud blasting norteño music. Streets are different yet same somehow. Many brown faces. A few white ones but not too many. Shī was expecting English, but this place is more Spanish. More Mexican. Maybe I'm not in America yet, she thinks. But keeps walking to church. Shī goes to first building that looks like church. It is white with big wooden cross on steeple. Has to be it, she thinks. Tries door. It is locked. Hears footsteps. Older woman with glasses answers door. Opens it just a bit, enough for half her face.

"Can I help you?" woman says.

"No habla ingles. habla español?" Shī asks.

"Si, mija. ¿Que quieres?"

"Estoy buscando Say-cri-ed Heart."

"¿Usted es inmigrante, mija?"

Shī nods head while woman explains where to go. Strange, she thinks, she never opened door all the way. Just enough for her to talk. Then shut it hard and fast. Walks past two buildings until she rounds corner and sees six big tents with giant air conditioners making its plastics walls shake. Red Cross truck sits just past gate. TV news vans with names like Telemundo, Galavision, and Univision are at door where woman with blue vest tells her to go in. Woman in blue vest never gets off phone. Everyone speaking Spanish here. Shī walks into building where women with blue vests are everywhere. Clothes in piles. Tables with food. Tables with toothpaste, brushes, and deodorants. No one says anything to her at first, but then young girl with hair in bun walks up and says, "Hola. ¿Puedo ayudarle?"

Shī explains her story to girl with hair in bun. Long walks in desert. Riding on top of trains. Same shoes. Same clothes. Same everything for days. Girl with hair in bun tells her many things, some she doesn't understand. Shī knows Spanish but only a little. When she attempts to tell girl with bun in hair that she doesn't speak Spanish well, girl with hair in bun cuts her off. Girl with hair in bun shows her to room with small shower and plastic curtain. Shī smiles for first time in weeks. Girl with hair in bun tells her that she will have new clothes when she is done. Shī smiles again. Shī takes shower and sees new clothes on chair waiting for her. Shī puts on new clothes. Feels like new person. No longer dirty. No longer Shī. Girl with hair in bun comes around corner and asks, "Why no bra and panties?"

Look comes over her face that takes her back to the Shī she was before shower. Shī looks at girl with hair in bun and tells her that coyotes made her hang them from tree after… Girl with hair in bun looks horrified. Becomes speechless. Shī looks at girl and steps closer and tells her that it is okay. Shī smiles again because she took pill before. No baby.

#rapetreesarereal
iTELEGRAM

Haldon Cruces [Donna, TX] to Rowena Garza [Albquerque, NM]

Message:
I heard a strange sound when I was on the road. {stop} It was night, and I was somewhere around King Ranch. {stop} I was definitely south of Sarita checkpoint. {stop} Had pulled over to take a piss and thought I heard a woman scream. {stop} Didn't know exactly what it was. {stop} At first I thought it was a coyote or maybe a goat. {stop} But deep down I knew it was something horrible. {stop} I contemplated whether I should check it out. {stop} My conscience told me that I had to check, so I did. {stop} I zipped up and turned on the flashlight app. {stop} At first I thought I saw the shadow of three people run across the darkened brush. {stop} Maybe it was the ghosts of immigrants that never quite made it. {stop} But I knew better. {stop} Walked up to the barbed wire fence. {stop} I knew it was ranch land and private property but the sounds of a woman crying forced me to trespass. {stop} What I saw, Row, was worse than anything I could have imagined. {stop} First I saw a tree with strange leaves. {stop} The woman was lying on the ground wearing only a shirt. {stop} No pants, not panties, just a pair of sandals and a white shirt with a pink ribbon on it. {stop} The shirt read, Help End Breast Cancer. {stop} Don't know why that is important, but it is. {stop} She looked at me and told me in

Spanish. {stop} "Leave me before they come back and kill you." {stop} I told her in my best broken Spanish that I had a car and I could take her where she needed to go. {stop} She looked at me, not ready to trust me. {stop} She hung her bra and panties from a tree and said. {stop} She couldn't go with me because the coyotes would find her and kill her. {stop} I explained that this is America and the Border Patrol are only a few miles up the road. {stop} "We can make it," I told her. {stop} She agreed, and she followed me back to my car. {stop} I turned to look one last time. {stop} Too many bras. Too many panties. Too many strange leaves. {stop} My heart was pounding waiting for the coyotes to jump out and kill us. {stop} But that never happened, she got in my car. {stop} I told her my name and asked hers. {stop} She told me her name was Shī, I didn't argue. {stop} We sped down the road to the checkpoint and I pulled over. {stop} Something I have never done and flagged down the first BP I could find. {stop} I told him my story and at first he didn't believe me. {stop} But then when she corroborated the story they took her inside the station. {stop} I was there 3 hours before they let me go. {stop} I asked what was going to happen to her. {stop} BP guy told me that she was going to be processed and probably let go. {stop} I couldn't believe my ears. {stop} I thought for sure they would deport her. {stop} But BP guy told me no because she was the victim of a crime. {stop} She gets a special visa and gets to see a judge. {stop} Crazy right? I didn't know. {stop} I got to speak to her one last time and then I gave her my card. {stop} Told her I lived in McAllen and if she needed anything. {stop} Don't know if I will ever see her again but at least. {stop} I did my good deed for the day. {stop} Catch you later Row, write back as soon as you get this. {stop}

#roadisalwaysbumpyanddark

Shī doesn't know what to do. Road is bumpy. Back of van is backed so tight, legs are starting to cramp from not being able to move. Shī closes her eyes and hopes ride is almost over. How many in here, she asks herself. Too many, she answers. Maybe ten, maybe more. Shī is only young girl by herself in this van. Others are mother and grandmother's age. Shī was sent alone. Mother didn't want her back home. Shī was fourteen about to be fifteen. Men on streets back in Guatemala starting to notice growing breasts on chest. Ass being shaped by growing hips. Thinning face and fuller lips. Mother tells her she is becoming a woman now. Shī thought she was woman when turned thirteen she bled for first time. Men didn't look at her then. Now when body aging faster than mind. Now Shī is woman.

Shī looks around darkened van. No real seats. No windows. Just smell of people sardined. At first, it bothered her. Now, she doesn't even smell anymore. Other groups almost all made up of kids her age. This group is mostly grandfathers, mothers without children, and young men with fear in eyes and hope in heart. One woman asks if she is scared. Shī thinks it is strange question. "Aren't we all?" she replies. Woman whose name is Benita Gomez-Santander touches her shoulder and smiles. Smile is most distraught she has ever seen. "No," she says, "Are you scared of these men and what they are going to do to you?" Shī has not really thought of it. She knew what the unspoken penalty was going to be, so she puts thought out of mind. For sanity. Shī asks Benita, "Are you scared?"

Benita looks at her and smiles again. This time the way a mother looks at daughter knowing that something terrible is coming and she can't stop or protect her. "Mijita," Benita says, "This isn't my first ride."

Shī just looks down, and Benita just holds her until van stops and sound of car doors opening and closing is heard. Benita then puts something in her hand and says, "Take this."

Shī is confused and doesn't react, so Benita looks her dead in eye and says, "Take it, por favor, now!"

Shī only has swallow left of water, and so she does as Benita asked. She swallows pill. Tastes bitter. Benita hugs one last time and says, "No baby. Not for you."

She feels hot tear trickle down Benita's cheek and onto her forehead.

#refugeegirlatmydoorstep

Rowena Garza: Yeah?

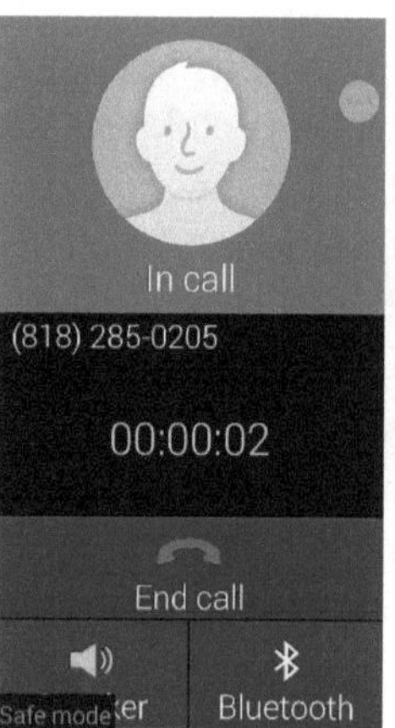

Haldon Cruces: Dude, I need your help.

Rowena: What's going on, man?

Haldon: You remember that telegram I sent you about the girl
I rescued?

Rowena: Yeah, that was weird.

Haldon: Well, she's here.

Rowena: Wait, what do you mean she's there?

Haldon: She's here at my house.

Rowena: How'd she find you?

Haldon: I gave her my card.

Rowena: Why'd you do that?

Haldon: I don't know. I just did.

Rowena: Well now she's your problem.

Haldon: Thanks, I know that.

Rowena: How old is she?

Haldon: I don't know, thirteen maybe. Why?

Rowena: Because you're a thirty-five-year-old man. Recently divorced. With an underage immigrant girl in your apartment.

Haldon: Dude, I'm not a pedophile. She's a kid.

Rowena: I know that. But the rest of the world ain't gonna see it that way.

Haldon: Row, help me here.

Rowena: Alright, Hal, honey. I don't know what you should do. Is there a social worker you can call?

Haldon: The social worker dropped her off here.

Rowena: The social worker drove her to your house? Why would they do that?

Haldon: Because all she had on her was my business card.

Rowena: Why would you put your home address on your business card anyway? You're a writer. There are a lot of *Misery* creeps out there.

Haldon: Rowena focus.

Rowena: Alright already. Tell the social worker you can't take her in.

Haldon: I did that already. Vanessa told me she had nowhere else to go. She has no family here.

Rowena: Okay, whose Vanessa?

Haldon: The social worker.

Rowena: Oh okay. Ummm....I don't know, honey. You are in uncharted territory here. What are the girl's options?

Haldon: Going to a detention center somewhere deep in the Midwest or…

Rowena: Or what?

Haldon: Staying here.

Rowena: You want to take care of this girl, don't you?

Haldon: I don't know.

Rowena: I hear it in your voice. She is not your problem. You did more than anyone can expect. You rescued that girl.

Haldon: But I feel responsible for her.

Rowena: Oh Hal. You and your conscience. They always get you in trouble.

Haldon: What do I do?

Rowena: You already took her in, didn't you?

Haldon: [silence]…yes, I did.

Rowena: Then why you calling?

Haldon: You know why.

Rowena: I'm your friend, not your mother or your wife. You don't need my permission.

Haldon: Just your support.

Rowena: You always have that.

Haldon: What now?

Rowena: I don't know, honey. I'll be down for the holidays. Keep me posted. Ciao.

Haldon: Yeah, later.

Rowena: Hit me up on Facebook. Give me progress report pics.

Haldon: Yeah, I will.

#journeybeginswith5thousand$$

Shī hates Mama because she took all their money. Everything. Took it and gave it to man with busy beard. Breathe like cerveza and eyes that always undress her. Mama says Guatemala is no place for indias bonitas. No place for young girls like Shī. Not anymore. Shī asks, what about her, but Mama says, Shī was more important. Go to U.S., Mama says. Go to U.S. and have better life. Coyote tells Mama that all Shī has to do is get across Mexican border, turn self into U.S. Migra and Shī would be free to be American. He also wants 5 thousand dollars American and a night with Mama. He wanted night with Shī, but Mama won't have it. Threatens to cut off huevos with butcher knife if he tries. Don't know how Mama will protect when Shī is on road with him. Don't know if Mama lets that thought invade. Don't think she wants it to. She cries all night before truck showed up. 4 am. 20 others in back of old truck. Shī doesn't want to leave Mama. Mama is all Shī has left. Papa was killed by gang coming home from mines one night. At least that is what Mama thinks. One night Papa just never came home. That was two weeks ago. Mama struggled to pay for both of them with waitressing and making pan dulce, but not enough. Never enough. Don't know how Mama gets money to pay Coyote. When asked, Mama refuses to tell. Has something to do with man who owns restaurant where Mama works. Shī wants to cry when she got on truck. Mama sees it on her face. But doesn't cry. Mama is always strong. But just before truck pulls away Shī sees single tear fall from corner of Mama's eye glistening in moonlight.

La Politiquera's Daughter

Sandra Acaña slammed her Toyota Prius door so hard it shook the whole car. She was angry at the meeting she had just had. She walked into her Palm Boulevard home looking out onto the Resaca and plopped herself down on her Italian leather sofa, crossing her arms across her chest and began to cry.

Mario heard the front door fly open, and he knew that the meeting didn't go well. He walked from the back office and saw his sister sitting on their overly extravagant couch crying and stated the obvious, "Didn't go too well, huh?"

Through her sobs, she said, "No shit, Sherlock."

"What happened with the professor?" Mario asked as he made his way to sit next to her on the couch.

"He was totally…weird. All he wanted to do was talk about Mom," she said wiping the tears from her face.

"Well, he did have her as a student, and she did talk about him, A LOT!" Mario said holding out a tissue he had grabbed when he heard the door open so violently.

"No, not that way. You know what he told me?"

"What?"

"He told me that Mom should be my manager. Can you believe that? Mom. He didn't even know she was dead. He said," she said looking at her brother's face, "He said he just saw her two days ago. He said that she was the one who set the meeting when I clearly emailed him."

"Oh, maybe he was just…"

"No, he was crazy, alright. He's not going to work. We need someone else."

Mario reached over and hugged her. "Sandy," he said in a low voice, "there isn't anyone else. You said no to everyone else."

"They were all misogynistic assholes. They just wanted to put me in short skirts and low tops and fuck me."

"Well, the professor was our last resort. I just filed your paperwork to run for county commissioner this morning. We are in for real now."

Sandra put her head down and said, "This wasn't supposed to be me. This was supposed to be Mom. She wanted this, not me."

Mario released her and picked her head up to look into her eyes, "Then why did you do this?"

"Because I made a promise to Mom."

"She never asked you to do this. To run for County Commissioner, she wanted you to be in Congress."

"Yeah, but this is the first step."

"Then we need the Professor."

Sandra rolled her eyes and said, "Mario, you weren't there. It was weird."

"But he is good. We worked on several campaigns for congressmen and even the Betty Lynch campaign. He is what we need, crazy or not."

Sandra looked back at her brother and smiled, "Why don't you be my manager? You are what I need."

"And I will be here with you every step of the way, but I can't manage you. I am a twenty-two-year-old artist who has no political savvy what-so-ever. And…and I'm gay. That will not play well here in the Valley. You need the Professor."

"He said he saw her two days ago."

"Maybe he did. I mean they never found her body."

Starting to get upset again she said, "Mario, don't start that again. She's gone. Alright. She went to Mexico and they got her, did things to her, and killed her. They found her car. Her blood on the seat and her torn panties. Just because they never found her body, doesn't mean she somehow survived and is living somewhere in Mexico with amnesia or something. This isn't a novella. This is real life. She's dead in a field somewhere."

Mario listened to the vitriol coming out of her mouth and didn't let it get to him because if he did, then he didn't know if he could handle it. "I know you are upset, but you don't have to be so mean."

Sandra, feeling a little bit guilty, turned away from him and looked at the floor, "Sorry, it's just…I miss her…"

Mario held her again and they both cried together.

Alejandro Leyva sat at his office computer typing away furiously. He had his first breakthrough in his novel in years, and it was all due to Melly Palacios. She had given him a story he could never have dreamt up and he couldn't wait to show it to her when it was done.

knock. knock.

Alejandro looked up from his laptop screen and saw a young man with an Art Matters T-shirt on. He was dark-skinned with jet-black hair and very thin. There was something familiar about him, but he couldn't quite place him.

"Dr. Leyva? May I speak with you a moment, if you are not too busy?"

Alejandro leaned back in his chair and said, "Sure, come on in. Are you a student of mine?"

"No, my name is Mario Acaña, I am Sandy's brother."

The name didn't quite click with him for a second but then

the lightbulb went off, and he said, "Oh Sandra, Melly's daughter. You must be her son."

"Yes, that's me," Mario said chuckling a little bit.

"Look, if this is about the meeting I had with your sister, please tell her how sorry I am for what happened. I didn't know your mother had passed. I am very sorry for that."

Mario thought he sound sane. "That's no problem. I knew it had to be some sort of confusion. My sister is going through a tough time right now. I mean she is running for Nelda Baca's seat and…"

"…she has zero political experience," Alejandro finished his thought.

"Well, she was President of the Student Government Association in college and President of the Creative Writing Club as well," Mario said and then realizing that Alejandro was not amused said, "but yeah, no she doesn't."

"Mario, I will be her manager. I will, but does she know you're here?"

Mario smiled and knew the gig was up, "No, she doesn't but she needs you, the other guys were total douchebags."

"Listen, I will do this but she has to meet me again and this time she has to be on time. You can come with her if you like, but I need to apologize to her in person."

Mario, surprised with the fact that he was so willing to help ,said, "Yes, I will get her there. Thank you. She really needs this."

"Make sure she is on time."

"Yeah, she's not so good at that."

"Dora's at noon on Friday."

Mario drove home to deliver the news in person to his sister because a text wouldn't suffice. He was ecstatic that the guy wasn't *Silence of the Lambs* creepy. He seemed like a nice guy. Mario, for the first time in a long time, felt like things were turning around for his family. She might actually win this thing. That would make Mom so proud, he thought and then immediately felt a dull ache in the pit of his stomach as he realized she wasn't here anymore.

"I got you another meeting with Dr. Leyva."

"You did what?" Sandra asked, sounding a little upset but happy at the same time.

"Yeah, he said he would do it. He wants to be your manager, but he wants to meet you Friday at noon at Dora's."

"Again. Friday at noon. That's weird."

"He didn't seem weird at all. He seemed really nice. He even said he wanted to apologize to you for what happened. See, things are turning around."

"Maybe, but still we have a long road ahead."

"He wants you there on time though," Mario slipped in under his breath.

"What does that mean?" Sandra was a little hurt by that.

"I mean you are not a very punctual person."

Taken aback, she stood there with her mouth open and said, "I am very often on time."

Mario shot her that look that he has when he knows she's lying.

"Well, I'm pretty much on time."

Mario held the look.

"Okay, okay. I will be on time. Are you coming with me?"

"No, I think you should do this yourself."

Sandra didn't know what to make of this news. She just knew that she had to keep this meeting. She was going to give Alejandro Leyva one more shot for her brother. She owed him that.

Sandra arrived ten minutes early for the first time in her life. She wore a dark blue top and slacks with her heels today. She didn't really like wearing skirts anyway. She just did that to test him the first time. She admired Hillary Clinton for rocking the pantsuit look. Sandra thought it was important for powerful women to wear pants to take that from the men as well. Alejandro Leyva showed up five minutes to noon, and he was dressed in a beat up fedora hat, a yellow short sleeve untucked shirt and blue jeans with scuffed up worker boots. He had a little bit of a gut but not enough to make him fat.

Alejandro sat down in front of her and said, "Sandra, I am so sorry for the last meeting we had. I didn't realize your mother was dead, and I don't want you to think that I am a creep or anything. I just admired your mother so much. She was a special lady."

Sandra felt a lot better about him now and said, "That's okay. I mean she was pretty great."

"So I will run your campaign, but I want to ask you first if you know what you are getting into. Who did you approach before you came to me? Santos?"

Sandra nodded.

"Rios?"

Another nod.

"Bobbie Martinez?"

Nod.

"Chevy?"

Nod.

"Those are all old school politicos. They know their stuff but.."

"…they're misogynistic pricks."

"I was going to say they are in the pockets of the Balli's."

Sandra rolled her eyes and said, "I know. I hate the fact that they control half of this county."

"So you know the key players?"

Feeling like she was being treated like a child, she said, "Of course, my mom's family has had a business here in Brownsville for fifty years. My mom used to drag me to all of her meetings with those assholes. She was always complaining that they were all about the mordida. They only care about lining their own pockets. They don't care about this city or the county. They only care about growing this place if it effects them, otherwise they find a way to shut it down. That's what I want to change. I want decent business people like my mom to get a shot at making this community better."

Alejandro smiled, "There is a politician in there. That's the fire you are going to need to win this thing. But you are at a disadvantage, you are an outlier. If you don't have the backing of the right people, your chances of winning are very low unless…"

"…unless I have a reputation and money from somewhere

else. I do, my mother has a great reputation in this town for being independent, and she was not afraid to stand up the Balli's, and when she.." clearing her throat, "when she died, she left me and my brother a sizable inheritance."

"How much are we talking?"

"Let's just say it is in the seven digits. My mom was a smart woman, she knew how to invest and the best insurance policy to get."

"Your mother was a powerhouse, wasn't she?"

"She was an amazing woman, and she taught me everything she knew since I was a kid."

"She wanted this for you, didn't she?"

"No, she wanted me to be president. She always said that. You will be president one day. But this, the county commissioner seat, this was her dream, and it's my start."

Alejandro flipped open his menu and said, "Before we get started here, let's eat."

Alejandro ordered a tuna on whole wheat and Sandra ordered a roasted turkey panini. Sandra had always grown up with money, but her mother always made her work for everything in life, and when she went the poet route, her mother was disappointed, but she still supported her. And when she came back home to open her own store, she was ecstatic, and Sandra knew that she was grooming her to be a politiquera again. Melly never gave up and Sandra knew it.

"So, why a discount clothing store and not a bookstore?" Alejandro asked her.

"Well, there's no money in books. I love books, I really do, and I think Brownsville certainly needs one, but it's a bad investment right now. Borders just went under. It's not a good time for books."

"You know that every election in this county is determined by 5,000 people. There are 100,000 people in Brownsville and about half a million in the county and only about five thousand of those vote in county elections. And it is always the same five."

"I know that, and that is why I think we need to target populations that don't usually vote. Like Southmost or something."

"Sandra, I am going to give it to you straight. You are a rich girl who grew up on Palm Boulevard. You went to St. Joe's. Have a graduate degree and your Spanglish ain't all that great. Those people are not going to vote for you. Some might because you are an attractive woman, but that only goes so far, but most importantly, those people do not vote."

"You know that is a very cynical way of looking at things. I think they haven't been given any hope. I can do that."

"Not in nine months you can't. You have to play the game as it is laid out before you. We have to play the cards we are dealt and we are dealt the local business card and you should use that," Alejandro put down his sandwich and touched her arm which was laying on the table, "I'm sorry to say this but we are going to have to use your mom to win this."

Sandra froze mid-bite and swallowed hard. She didn't know if she could do that. She had not talked publically about her mother, and she didn't know if she could. "I don't know if I can do that."

"Her story and what happened to her is horrible. I know. I feel horrible asking you to do this, but that will win you the sympathy you need to swing voters."

Sandra took a long sip of her water and said, "I don't know. I'll think about it."

Mario sat in the living room looking over the poll numbers for Sandra and saw how much better she was doing with Dr. Leyva managing her, but she was still behind by six points. She was losing to Beto Canales, the sleazy city manager from Brownsville. He was definitely in the pocket of the Balli's, and that was giving him the edge. Mario knew what she had to do to take this over the top, but she refused to do it.

Sandra walked in and plopped herself down next to her brother and the stacks of papers surrounding him. "I'm exhausted. I just did the Literary Event for Kids and those kids are…well, let's just say that I don't want kids ever."

"Don't let the voters hear you say that. We need the parent

vote," Mario said never looking at her. He just kept his eyes locked on the pages in front of him.

"I know. I'm just venting to my little brother," she said kicking off her heels and putting her feet up on a stack of papers on the coffee table.

Mario didn't respond; he was just reading something intently.

"Mario," Sandra said, "talk to me. You've been so serious lately."

"We are one month from the election and you are still six points behind."

"I know, but Alejandro says that's not bad, we can turn it around."

"How?"

"He says he has an ace up his sleeve."

"What does that mean? Is he gonna give cocaine for votes?"

"Mario, of course not, but I trust him. He's gotten us this far."

"What about that other thing? That thing he asked you to do."

"I can't do it. I can't use Mom that way."

"But it will win us an election."

"No, I won't use Mom that way, and that's that. You sound like Alejandro."

"Because he's right."

Sandra sighed and decided to change the subject, "Have you seen Alejandro? He's disappeared again."

"He wasn't with you at the Literacy thing?"

"No, it's Friday. You know, he always disappears on Fridays."

"I always do these Friday events on my own because you won't come out with me."

"Sandy, I will only hurt your campaign out there."

"Why? Because you are gay? Everyone knows that."

"Yes, they might, but they don't want to be reminded about it."

"Alright, alright. But what do you think he does on Fridays? Maybe he's Jewish or something?"

"What?"

"You know Jews have that Sabbath thing where they can't leave their house for like a whole day."

"That's Saturdays, and I don't think he's Jewish."

"Then what?"

"I don't know. Why don't you follow him?"

"I can't. I am on the campaign trail. I have too many things to do, but…" she said smiling at him in that way she does when she wants him to do something for her.

"No, I can't. I mean I've got too much work to do here."

"Oh come on, I have to know, and it's only one Friday. Come on, please?"

Mario couldn't believe he was doing this. He was staked out on a bench outside of Alejandro's office. He saw him go in about an hour ago, and he was just sitting here feeling like a spy with the dark sunglasses and everything. Then after about another thirty minutes he saw Alejandro walking out with a woman that from this distance looked at least ten years older than him. They seemed to be laughing and enjoying themselves but then he realized they were headed right for him, so he got up and ran into the nearest building which was the library. He waited for them to pass and then started to follow them again. He stayed about fifty yards behind like he had read on the Internet when he googled: how to follow someone like a professional spy. He followed them to a coffee house and stayed outside as to not tip them off that he was following, but after an hour or so, he got hungry and quickly ran to the closest fast food joint and got the greasiest thing he could find. This was a one-time thing he told himself. He came back twenty minutes later and saw that they were still there. They stayed there for hours, and Mario was getting bored just waiting here. Being a spy sucks, he thought to himself, so much just waiting around. But then he saw them leave the coffee house and make their over to a restaurant and then he got a closer look at the woman. For a second he didn't know if what he saw was real, so he blinked really hard and looked again. His jaw dropped and the word, "Mom," fell out of his mouth.

Mario didn't know how to confront them. He just watched them laugh, kiss by a resaca, and go up to his office and do God knows what, but he did think he saw a silhouette of two people having sex. He didn't want to think about it because if this was his mom, then that was just wrong. They came out of the building around one in the morning. Mario could not believe he had just waited that long but the realization of seeing his mom again was just too much to let go of now, and he had to confront them now or never, he thought.

As they headed for the parking lot where there were only a couple cars left, he caught up to Alejandro but his mother was gone. "Alejandro!" He yelled out.

Alejandro startled by hearing a voice call out his name jumped a little and turned around to see Mario. "Mario, what are you doing here?"

"I was just about to ask you the same thing."

"I was just picking up some papers."

"Who was that woman? The one you were with?"

"Who? It's just me."

"No, I saw her. I have been following you all day. Is it...?" he couldn't finish his sentence.

"Mario, please...let me explain."

"Is it her? Is it my mother?"

"Mario, please...calm down. I can explain."

Mario listened to the story that Alejandro laid out for him, and he felt like he was insane. How could any of this be true? It was like he was in an episode of the *Twilight Zone*. Things like this don't happen.

"I want to see her. I want to see my mom."

"You can't. She's gone."

"You see her every fucking Friday."

"Yes, I know, but she won't be back until.."

"Next Friday."

"Yes."

"And it's only Fridays?"

"Yes, only on Fridays. That's the only day I get to see her. I love her."

"You love her? How can you love a dead woman?"

"I love her, and she's not dead to me."

"You have ghost sex with her. How is that by the way? I know that's weird because it's my mom and all but it's not any weirder than anything you've told me tonight."

"It's real. She feels so real. I can't explain it."

"How long have you been seeing here? And I mean that in every possible way."

"Since the day before I met with your sister for the first time."

"Are you going to tell Sandy?"

"No, she can't know. Not yet. Not until she wins. This will break her."

"I don't know if I can keep this from her. I mean lying to her is hard, she always knows."

"Then don't lie. Just tell her I am seeing a woman but don't tell her who."

"I don't know. This is massive."

"Just until the election and then you can tell her everything. Please."

Mario looked at him. "Can I at least see her next week?"

"Mario, I don't know if that's a good idea. She really wants Sandra to win, and if you see her, she might not come back and then I don't know what will happen."

Mario started to feel tears stream out of the corner of his eyes. "I need to see her. Please let me see her."

"The night of the election. I promise."

"That's two weeks away. I don't know if I can wait that long."

"Two weeks and then you can see her."

Mario wiped the tear away, "Okay, but how are we going to win this election? Beto is too far ahead. He has all the right backing."

"I've taken care of it. She will win this thing, only if she doesn't know about this. We don't want her off her game right now."

"What have you done?"

"You'll see on election night. Just stay with her. She needs you now more than ever."

"And what about you? She needs you too."

"I've done what I can for her. She has to finish this on her own."

It was 8:59 pm on election night and the numbers were coming in big for Sandra. Mario sat while she watched intently from their living room. Her volunteers were all around her cheering. Alejandro stood by the TV looking like he was lost in thought. She was winning this thing, and they just needed a few more districts to make her win official. Mario watched from the kitchen, alone. He had kept quiet about Alejandro and his mom for two weeks and tonight was the night he was going to be able to see her. And then Sandy jumped up and started screaming. Mario cracked a half smile; Alejandro had done it. He had won this thing for her. Whatever the bastard did, it worked. He had not seen her this happy since before their mom died. Mario was so happy. Sandra rushed to him and hugged and kissed him. "We did it," she said.

"Yes, we did. Now, you have to make your speech. They are all waiting for you on the front lawn."

"Come on, let's go." She said as started to walk toward the front door.

"I'm right behind you," Mario looked over to Alejandro who was looking right at him.

Mario walked over to Alejandro who looked happy and sad at the same time. But you could only see the sadness if you looked for it and Mario did. "Well, this is it. She won. Whatever you did worked. Now, I want to see my mother."

"I know, and she's waiting for you," Alejandro pointed outside toward their backyard. Melly was standing there looking so happy. She smiled at Mario and he walked over to her. He opened the sliding glass door and walked out to her.

Alejandro watched as she embraced her son. She looked over at him and he looked at her and said, "I love you." She mouthed it back and then they were gone.

Alejandro pulled a manuscript from under his jacket. It was held together with a big black binder clip and on the cover was stapled a newspaper that read: Local Business Woman and Son Disappear in Mexico.

Alejandro walked out to see Sandra making her acceptance speech. He smiled at her and she looked back and smiled at him. He knew he had to tell her tonight, but he wanted her to enjoy the victory just a little longer.

THE BLACK BOX

Curly looked at that black box and could not understand why someone would protect several wirebound notebooks in a heavy-duty lockbox. It needed a combination and a key to open it. It took Curly days to figure out how to get it open, and that was all that was inside. He couldn't understand it. He couldn't go back to the gang with this and hope to be the newest Loco Brown Bomber. Being an LBB was all he wanted. He was fifteen years old and his older brother, David, was an LBB serving time at Beeville. His father he never knew. His mother walked out on him and his brother when she met a guy who didn't want kids. All of the Zamorra's were being raised by their grandmother, who worked 60 hours a week as a nurse at the local hospital. Curly was now the man of the house because David was locked up and he had to be an LBB to prove he was a man. He had never been the strongest, fastest, or coolest kid in school but he was liked by most.

Ramon was the leader of the local LBB's, and David's best friend growing up. He had agreed to look after Curly while David was in the pen and he quickly took him under his wing and groomed him to be a Loco Brown Bomber. Ramon was like a father to Curly, and all he wanted was Ramon's respect, but now he had screwed up his initiation. He had stolen a black safe filled with 99 cents notebooks. What was he going to do with those? Why were they in this box? Where is the money? The jewelry? Something more valuable than notebooks filled with writing.

"What you got there, ese?" Ramon said from behind Curly.

Curly quickly closed up the box and turned around to see Ramon with a joint hanging out his mouth and a Bud in his hand. "Nothing, just some junk 'buelita wanted me to throw out." Ramon said, "Orale, come in here and smoke some of this shit; it's da bomb."

Curly followed Ramon into the converted garage, which was the gang headquarters, Ramon's bedroom in his mother's house. In the room were two other guys and a chola with the painted eyebrows, tat's, and a tiny tank top with boobs spilling out all over. That was Ricky, short for Enriqueta. She was always hanging around. Sometimes she would take a ride with the homeboys and take part, but mostly she was Derek's girl. They were always fucking in the broken down van in the front lawn. Everyone could hear them and Curly would always be sent in to clean up the condom wrappers and stains left behind that he didn't want to know about. The other guy was Chuy; he was Derek's best friend and the most vicious vato in the gang. He had just got out for assault; luckily the cops never found the pipe he used or else he would have gotten serious time for assault with a deadly weapon. But Chuy only served 18 months in county, and now he had to wear one of those ankle monitors. He couldn't go 50 yards from his house. Luckily, he lived right next door, which in the barrio is only ever five feet from any neighbor.

"So, Curly, have you done it yet? Your initiation?" Derek asked as he took a big drag and passed it to Ricky.

"Nah, not yet, pues I found this couple that just moved into that new subdivision down the road. I will check that place out today."

Ramon grabbed Curly's shoulder and said, "No rush, don't want you to get caught on your first B&B."

Ramon always looked out for Curly in a way that he didn't for the other guys. Sometimes Curly thought Ramon didn't exactly want him in the gang life. He had postponed his initiation twice now. "No, I'll do it today. Just you wait, I'll have something good tonight."

"Órale, little holmes."

Shī sat in the library at a back table where no one would bother her. She was reading Pablo Neruda's *Book of Odes* bilingual edition slowly because she really wanted to learn both languages but English was a lot harder than Spanish. Growing up in her village back home she had heard Spanish spoken around, and English was only on signs and Cokes. She had been in the U.S. for only a year now, and her English had gotten a lot better, but she still mixed words up. Hal, her guardian, gave her all of these bilingual poetry books to try and help her learn English, and she was trying. She really was, but the classes were mostly in English, and that was hard. So, she practiced every chance she got. Shī noticed him hiding behind the realistic fiction section, staring at her. His name was Curly, or at least that is what they called him. Shī knew that he liked her in a way, and she tried to stay away from him because he was always hanging around the gang kids. She knew all about gangs and did not want anything to do with them. She remembered what they did to her.

Curly had so many ideas in his head about how to approach her, but he shot down every single one of them. He chose stalking behind bookcases and watching her from a distance as the best approach. He had liked Shī ever since she arrived at their school a year ago. She was really smart; he knew this because she was always reading. She didn't talk much in class or to anyone really.

She was a loner, and he liked that about her. She was beautiful to him. She was thin, but her chi-chi's were big. She had skin lighter than his, but her hair was blacker than anything he had ever seen. And it was straighter than any other girl in school. She had very india features as his abuela would say. And she was tall for her age. She also had a cute accent he knew wasn't Mexican. She was Guatemalan; he knew that because she had come in during that summer when all those kids came to Valley, and there was a big stink from the gringos up north.

"Curly?" a voice broke his deep fantasy about him and Shī kissing.

"Huh?" was all he could muster up as a response.

"Are ju looking at me?" Shī said tired of him staring at her from behind the bookshelves.

"Uh, no, well umm," he didn't know what to say. He was caught off guard, and now she was talking to him. She had never really talked to him before ever. And she knew his name!

"Did you want something? It just weird you look at me like that," Shī said feeling uncomfortable.

"Sí, Shī, I umm, wanted to know what you're reading," Curly fumbled out the words with the first thing that came to mind.

"It's poems."

Curly came out from behind the stacks and walked over to her. "You like poetry?"

"Yes, Hal loves it, and since it bilingual, it help me learn English and Spanish," Shī didn't know why she told him all that.

"Who's Hal?" Curly started to feel jealous about this other guy.

"He is my American father."

"Oh, okay," Curly felt better, "You're from Guatemala, right?"

"Yes."

"How is it over there?"

"Not good, I have to come here and escape the violence."

Curly realized what a stupid question that was now that she answered, but he was so nervous that he didn't know what to say. "Oh, yeah, that's right. I'm sorry about that, chica."

Shī looked confused and asked, "Why you call me chica? That not my name."

Curly realizing he had slipped into mocho-speak said, "No, it's something we call girls here, like…um…"

"…like honey or sweetie?"

"Yeah, like that but Mexican, you know?"

Shī sat up and made herself stiff like a board. "Well, my American mother says that you shouldn't call girls things like that because…how she say it…monikers like girl, sweetie or honey demean us as women and reinforce pay-tree-archy. Yes, I think that right."

Curly was stunned, he had never heard anyone talk that way. He liked her even more now. But at the same time he had no idea what she was talking about. He just knew that she didn't like being called 'chica'. "I'm sorry," he said, "I didn't know it was bad to call you that. I won't do it again."

"Okay," Shī said feeling sorry for him now. He was just trying to make conversation and Shī felt bad about correcting him, but her American mother had always told her to correct anyone who tries to treat her like an object. "Sorry, I just get… how you say it…worked out."

"Worked up."

"Yes, worked up," Shī was starting to like him a little better now. He didn't seem like those other gang kids. He was sweet and since she really didn't have friends, so she said, "Did you want to sit with me?"

Curly felt a hard-on coming on, and he had to adjust his pants a little. He didn't ever expect for her to talk to him and now she was inviting him to sit. "Yes," he said after a few seconds of staring off into the space of shock and amazement.

Curly sat down with her and they talked. Shī seemed to like him, once he dropped the tough guy act and just talked to her. He found out about her American father, who took her after he rescued her from the coyotes, and that her American father wasn't married to her American mother because she lived in Albuquerque, but she came back to the Valley every month or so. Shī also told him that her American mother was once a man and now was a woman. Curly didn't know if she said that right but he just let her talk. She talked much more than he had ever heard her talk. It was like she was a faucet that was only ever opened to a drip and then someone came along and opened it all the way and now the water was really flowing. The bell rang and Curly offered to walk her to her class. Shī agreed and Curly smiled. He was getting somewhere now and maybe Shī would be his girlfriend.

Curly looked at the black box of notebooks again and this time took the spiral notebooks out and started to read them. They were filled with poetry and notes. The poems were mostly hard for Curly to understand, so he downloaded a dictionary app on his phone and used it every time he came across a word he didn't know. He even bought one of those little notebooks from the dollar store and started to write down all the words he didn't know. He wanted to impress Shī, now that she was talking to him. Some of the poems really spoke to him. He never knew that someone else felt the same about being different, and they expressed it in poetry that didn't sound anything like that Robert Frost guy or even that Shakespeare he could never understand. This stuff was talking about real life.

"Hey, Curly, what you reading?"

Curly shut the notebook like his abuela had just caught him masturbating. "What?"

"What you got there?" It was Derek; he was already buzzing at ten in the morning.

"Nothing, just some school shit."

"Then why you hiding it like some porn shit?"

"Naah, I was just you know…startled…"

Derek looked confused for a second and then took a hit off of his joint and said, "Startled? I don't think I ever heard a vato use that word."

Curly blushed a little and said, "It's something from one of the books I'm reading. It means…"

"I know what it means, whatever bro, you want a hit?" Derek extended his half-smoked joint to Curly.

Curly shook his head and said, "Naah, I got to be somewhere." He jumped up, put the notebook back in the black box and walked out with the box under his arm. Curly stopped before he completely exited the garage and looked back at Derek smoking and drinking a beer and for the first time he thought, I don't want to be that old and still hanging out in my abuela's garage. He turned and walked out.

Curly met Shī at the Placita, which was a central park in an old part of the city. The jungle gym was all metal and the ground was all concrete. The basketball hoops never had a net and there was graffiti everywhere, but it was a good place to meet since it was the middle ground between Shī's house and his abuela's. She showed up with a copy of a book by a Chicana writer writing about the Lost Girls of Juarez. Shī read some poems from it, and Curly really liked them. He had copied down some poems in his little notebook from the black box and recited them to her. She seemed to like them. He told her that they were his and immediately he knew that it was wrong but he wanted to impress her, so he held to the lie. Shī told him that her real name was Shīchihuitchilique Zapotecoyotl but in Guatemala the government called her "Shī Zapoteca" and that is the name that she always used. Curly tried to say her real name, but he failed miserably after several attempts and Shī laughed at him every time. Curly thought he should have been embarrassed but he made a game of it, and they both enjoyed it.

They talked for about an hour about Curly's brother in prison and his wanting to be in the LBB, but when he started to talk about the gang, Shī turned cold and said, "I don't want nothing to do with gangs. Gangs did bad things to me and my mother." Curly tried to explain to her that the LBB wasn't like that, but she wouldn't listen. She didn't like gangs, so he didn't talk about that with her.

They talked about movies instead, and she had seen a lot of movies he had never seen. Movies that were independent as she called them and a lot of gay films she watched with her American mother and her kids. But the one thing that she really loved was Star Trek: The Next Generation, not the old one or the one where they are lost in space but the one with Data. She loved Data because she saw a lot of herself. Shī did not understanding everything like him, but at the same time, he seemed so much more loveable than any of the others. Curly had only seen the new Star Treks and knew he had to Netflix that series. It was old, from the '90s or something, but Shī made it sound so good.

When the sun started to go down, Shī said she had to go home or Hal would be worried, and Curly offered to walk her home. Shī accepted, and he walked her to an old house on Miller Street that still had a window unit AC hanging out the front window. It had a big fence and gate around it. It had a carport and a weird ramp to the front door that Shī explained was used when Hal's grandfather used to live here, and he was old and couldn't move too well. When they got to the gate, Curly could see someone inside cooking dinner, and it smelled good.

"So?" Curly said looking into her eyes.

"Yes?" Shī said starting to blush and knowing that he wanted to kiss her and she wanted that too, but she had never kissed a boy before, and she didn't know who was supposed to go first.

"Can I kiss you?" Curly just blurted out feeling his heart almost jumping out of his chest.

Shī smiled, blushed even more, and said timidly, "Yes."

Curly leaned in and their lips touched for a few seconds before a voice called out, "Shī! Come inside. Dinner is ready."

Shī pulled back. She liked the kiss, but Hal startled her when he called her inside. Curly felt that movement in his pants again and had to adjust his pants so she wouldn't notice. He really liked the way her lips felt and just stood there stupidly watching her open the gate and then closing it as a weenie dog came up to her and started jumping all over her. She petted it and walked inside with it. Curly smiled all the way back home and thought about nothing but Shī and watching Star Trek.

When Curly got home, he saw several police cars outside of his house. Curly's heart dropped thinking that he was busted for stealing the black box, but he saw Derek and Chuy in handcuffs with Ricky crying with a cop. She had blood all over her face and Derek and Chuy were all beat up. Ramon was nowhere to be found until he looked in the back of one of the cruisers and saw Ramon there looking pissed and stone cold. Curly didn't know what to do. If he should go into the house or ask the guys what happened? But before he could make a decision, his abuela called out to him and told him to get in the house. Curly walked inside with his abuela and asked her several questions about what happened. She only said that she would explain everything when the cops left, but right now he had to stay in the house and be quiet. Curly watched from the kitchen window that looked out toward the garage as the cops put Derek and Chuy in the back of their cruisers and left. Ricky was taken away by the ambulance. Curly went to his room and opened up the laptop his brother had bought him before he went to prison and started watching Star Trek: The Next Generation. The incident in his front lawn might have bothered him if it didn't happen all the time here. His abuela never told Curly anything, but he knew that when Ramon got out he would give him the scoop.

Curly stayed up to about three in the morning watching most of the first season of Star Trek, and he liked it, but he thought the special effects were cheesy compared to the CGI stuff that the new movies have. But the stories were good and he liked Wharf the best. He was awesome. Troi was super hot and even Yar, but they killed her off real quick.

The next day, Ramon was released and he told Curly that it was just a thing about Ricky being a bitch and Derek got mad and Chuy stepped in to defend and it just got out of control. Curly just listened to Ramon and nodded his head but he knew the real story. Ricky was jealous of Derek because him and Chuy were always going into the van together. Even though Chuy said he liked girls, he caught Chuy on his knees sucking off Derek once late at night. Curly couldn't help it; they did it right outside his bedroom window at three in the morning. When Ramon told the story, he decoded the real story that Ricky found Chuy sucking off Derek and she just went ballistic, beating on both of them and then Derek, being the vato loco he is, hit her back hard. She had a fractured jaw. Curly had never liked guys, but he never really thought there was anything wrong with it. He saw it all the time with Derek and Chuy, but they kept it on the down low. Curly liked girls for as long as he could remember and even though he thought about whether he would grow to like guys, he hadn't yet. And now that he found Shī, he could think of no one else. Ramon asked Curly about Shī and Curly said, "She's awesome, she's smart and funny and she has that great accent and…"

Ramon smiled and said, "Oh man, you got it bad."

"What?"

"You in love, carnal. First time, huh?"

"No, well, yeah…I guess so," Curly said trying to at first sound cool but then surrendering to his feelings.

"That's alright. Nothing to be ashamed. Everyone goes through that. But just remember one thing and this is speaking from experience. Use protection. Don't get her pregnant. That's a responsibility you don't want to have at your age."

"But you got two kids you had when you were fifteen," Curly said confused.

"Yes and I love both Raul and Soledad to death. Yo, I would die for them but if I had a chance to get myself right before I had kids I would do that and that is why I say that. Here," Ramon said handing Curly some crumpled up condoms he had in his pocket. "Use these every time you fuck her. Every time. You hear me?"

Curly took them and stuffed them in his pocket. "Thanks, Ramon."

"No problem, ese, but do you know how to use them?"

"You just slide them over your dick, right?"

"Yeah, but there's a little more to it than that. Here, let me show you. Go get a banana from the house."

Curly went and got a banana from the house and watched as Ramon demonstrated how to properly use a condom. The entire time that he watched Ramon put a condom on a banana, Curly thought, I am nowhere near that big but he didn't say that out loud.

Curly was nervous when he met up with Shī again. All he could think about was sex with Shī and how to use the condom right. He was hoping the condom wasn't too big for him. Shī met him at the library at lunch like they had been doing for a week now. But she didn't smile when she came over; she didn't look happy at all. She sat down at the table, opposite from him, and plopped down a small brown book on the table.

"You are a stealer," she said sounding very angry.

Curly had no idea what she was talking about and said, "What do you mean?" And then he thought, she knows about the black box.

"You stole those poems you said you wrote."

"How do you know that?" was all Curly could think of when she leveled that accusation at him.

"Those poems come from this book here. It was written by a poeta from here in the Valley. You just took her poems and told me they were yours. You are a stealer."

Curly knew he was busted and so told her the whole story about the initiation and the black box. Shī didn't seem to care at all. All she said was, "I thought you was a nice guy. I hate gangs. And what you did was wrong. You have to give that box back."

"But I love poetry now and Star Trek. I do."

Shī got up and said, "Goodbye. I never want to talk to you again."

Curly tried to stop her but it was too late. She was gone and he was left feeling horrible. The rest of the day Curly was in a daze trying to find a way to solve this problem. He didn't know what to do so he went home and spent the weekend watching all of Star Trek. It took all of the weekend but he did it and then he decided to do something.

Curly walked back to the house he had taken the black box from and he knocked on the door. A tall, dark-skinned woman answered the door.

"Yes," she said.

"About two weeks ago, I took this from outside your house as you were moving in. I am here to return it. I am sorry."

The woman looked at him for a second and then said, "Do you want to come in? I have agua fresca."

Curly nodded and went inside and the woman poured him a

glass and then asked him, "Why did you take it?"

Curly explained about his initiation and then told her his whole story about falling in love with Shī and his new interest in poetry and Star Trek. The woman just listened to his story as he talked and didn't say a word until he was done and then said, "Curly, have you started writing your own poetry?"

Curly lowered his head and looked down at his glass, "Yes, but it is not good."

"Share it with me."

"It's not good."

"Let me be the judge. Díme."

Curly took out his little notebook and read his poem about the color blue. It was only four lines but he had spent an hour writing it.

Blue
it breaths and feels
like a prisoner on his last day
right before the doors open
and it knows that all is holy

The woman nodded her head and said, "Chido, that was good. Let me tell a story. I was raised on Moody just like you. You know that burnt out lot down the road from the Placita?"

Curly nodded.

"That was my house when I was a little girl. But when that house burned down, we moved in with my rich uncle in McAllen. Everything in that house was expensive and we weren't allowed to touch anything. But one day my uncle shows me a book of poetry he wrote when he was young and it was at that moment that I knew that raza could write and have books. I never knew my uncle wrote and now he was showing me his poetry. I read it and fell in love with poetry from that point on. I was ten years old and I have spent my life studying and writing poetry. A lot of it is really bad but the good stuff I publish. But the story I want to tell is when I was twenty, my uncle told me that his college mentor was dying and that I should meet him before he dies.

He was an old-school Chicano who marched in all the marches and he became a professor to teach the raza how to organize and to inspire new generations of Chicanos. He wanted what the movement wanted: Chicanos succeeding. So Ernesto, my uncle, took me to his home which was nice but not as nice as my uncle's. He was pretty much bed-ridden and he needed one of those oxygen tanks to breathe. He smiled when he saw me and they talked about the old days, which I didn't know. They talked about all of the Chicanos in power and how many of them were corrupt. They were getting put in prison and removed like Sylvia Handy and others. And then he said something that I did not expect. He said that was his fault. That was the fault of all the old school Chicanos who mentored the younger ones back in the day. They taught all of these politicians, sheriffs, and D.A.'s and they taught them to do whatever it takes to get things done because things were already so stacked against them. Because that is what they had to do in the '60s. They had to do whatever it took and sometimes that meant doing the wrong thing. It was playing the game the only way they knew how, through bribes and intimidation…"

"…like the gangs," Curly interrupted.

"Yes, like gangs, dealers, and gangsters. And now they are all going to jail. They liked the money too much. They liked the power too much. They were acting like they had won the game, but the game isn't rigged for Chicanos, it is rigged against us. And the more they played the game with their rules, the more they became everything they said we were. And after this old-school Chicano was done, my uncle stood up and you know what he said?"

"No, what did he say?"

"He said, but you also made me. The young Chicano who did things right. Who fought the battle through poetry, through good business, through success," the woman paused for a second and looked at Curly who was deep in thought at this point.

"But what is a Chicano? How do I be one?"

"That is something you are going to have to learn for yourself. Keep reading books by raza. Read about our history through our words. But most of all, you have to drop this stupid gang shit and get that girl back, she will be your guide. She already seems like she is ahead of the game."

"But the LBB is all I ever wanted to be. I don't know how I get out."

"Do you know, when I was a kid, I was you. The painted eyebrows, the Dickies, the whole deal, but because of my uncle I left that all behind. That doesn't mean that being a chola is bad; it isn't. It just means you are choosing your own path. Look here, keep the box. I don't need it anymore."

"Are you sure? It's got personal stuff in there, too."

"Yes, I'm sure. It will do you more good than it will me."

Curly got up, apologized one more time, scooped up the box and left. He didn't know what to think about what just happened. He thought she was going to call the cops on him or yell at him or something but she didn't. She did something far worse. She opened his eyes to a different path.

Curly walked home contemplating everything she told him and then when he came up to his house, he saw the four LBB's sitting around the garage smoking weed and laughing. Derek and Chuy were out and even Ricky was in there too. Same old. Same old. Instead of walking into the garage and hanging with them like he usually did, he went inside and sat down with his abuela. The black box in between them.

POSTMODERN QUINCEÑERA

iTelegram
Haldon Cruces [Donna, TX] to Rowena Garza [Albquerque,
NM]

Message:
White. Salt. The salt is white. This is the first thing I noticed. The cake is white. The walls are white. {stop} The tablecloths, the napkins, everything except the people. {stop} The only brown things in this room. I usually wouldn't have noticed the contrast. {stop} But as Lorraine Hansberry once said, "You don't notice how black you are until you stand up against a white wall." {stop} That is so true in this space. We were in this place called Blana Negra. {stop} It is an extremely

expensive event hall. But this is Shī's quinceñera, and I think she deserves. {stop} A little normal after two years of being here. I think it was the U.S. school's influence. {stop} Shī swears she has to have one or she'll die. So, here I am dropping a couple grand. {stop} On a little girl's fifteenth birthday party. {stop} Need your help ASAP. {stop}

Rowena arrived three days after her semester ended. She was determined to have Shī's quinceñera before school let out so that her friends would all know about it. The thing was that I didn't know how many friends Shī had. She only really talked to a couple of girls, and only one had ever come to the house. Rowena had assured him over several telegrams that every kid loves a quinceñera. Free cake. Dancing. And it's a party. I was not as confident as she was but she was the woman, at least now she was.

"Are you listening to me?" Rowena said breaking me from my thoughts.

"Yeah, all kids love parties," I repeated, not really sure if that was what she said.

We were driving back from the Harlingen airport, her fifteen suitcases (she says I'm exaggerating, but I'm not) stuffed somehow in my backseat and trunk. Shī was still in school, and Rowena's arrival was to be a surprise for her. "Hal, you know this is every little Mexican girl's dream."

"How would you know? You were a little boy."

"Don't be a dick. I went to plenty of quinceñera's when I was young. Didn't you?"

I sat silent. I didn't want to tell her that I was not the popular kid. I never really got invited.

"Oh my God, you didn't go to any as a kid? You are so pocho," Rowena laughed.

"I went to my sister's and my cousins, but no, I was a loner back in those days," I refuted her accusation.

"Oooh, didn't mean to peel open an old wound. So where are we going now?" Rowena said, realizing we passed the exit to Donna.

"We have an appointment with the Congressman in Brownsville."

"Congresswoman," Rowena corrected me like she always did. I expected it, and I kind of liked it.

Sandra Acaña was the freshman representative from our area. She had spent the last nine years working her way up from City Council to Congresswoman. She was a friend of mine from way back. Well, a little more than friends but that was years ago. This was 2015, and my life had changed dramatically since my college days, and so had hers. I looked around the office we sat in waiting for Sandra to finish her meeting. I saw a picture of her with her two kids, a boy and a girl with a salt and pepper haired Alejandro Leyva. I had Dr. Levya for a writing class years ago, and he was a good teacher when he showed up because he was always gone working on some political campaign or another. I hadn't heard that Sandy and Dr. Leyva had married, but then I didn't really follow politics until Shī entered my life.

Sandra entered looking really good. She was wearing a navy blue blazer and matching skirt with black heels. She turned to Rowena and me and said, "Sorry to keep you waiting. I was with the SpaceTech people. They want to launch space shuttles out of Boca Chica beach. Isn't that crazy?" Sandra turned and saw Hal and said, "Hal, oh my God, it's you. It's been years. How are you?"

"I'm good." I could feel Rowena's jealousy piercing me, "this is Rowena, my partner...I mean girlfriend."

Rowena gave me that look like I knew I was in trouble. "Hi, I'm Dr. Rowena Garza."

Sandy sat down in her chair after shaking our hands and said, "It's good to meet you, and it's nice seeing you again, Hal. It's been since we got our MFA's together, years ago. You still writing?"

"Yeah, I am. I'm working on my second novel now."

"Oh, I didn't know you were published."

"Not many people do," I said trying to be funny.

"What's it called so I can pick up a copy?"

"It's called The Road to La Llorona Park..."

"…It's about us really," Rowena interrupted my very obvious flirting.

"Interesting," Sandy said writing down the name on a post it, "So, what can I help you with?"

"Sandy, as you know from my emails, I have taken in a refugee. She's Guatemalan, and we were wanting to adopt her because right now her legal status is still going through immigration court and we were wondering if you could help us expedite the process or something."

Sandy leaned back and looked at both of them. "You two aren't married, right?"

"No, we are not yet."

I could see Sandy stiffening up and she said, "I have to be honest with you, Hal. The way you got custody of She…"

"Shī, her name is Shī," I don't know why I corrected her but I felt I owed Shī that.

"…the way you got custody of Shī is strange, to say the least. How did that happen?"

"Shī requested to stay with me, and at the time, immigration was flooded with all of those unaccompanied minors, so when someone like me, who has a clean record, a job, and a house offered to foster her, they didn't argue."

"And Shī requested you because you rescued her?"

"Yes."

"Look, Congresswoman Acaña, Hal has spent the last two years caring for Shī, and this request is something that could be a huge win for you in the next election, which is right around the corner if I am not mistaken," Rowena interrupted us.

"I understand you really care for this girl, but what about her mother? What does she have to say about this?"

"I am in constant contact with Gisela Zapoteca, Shī's mother, and she has given her consent. And that is actually something else you might be able to help me with. Shī is going to have her quinceñera in about a month, and I know Shī would really love it if her mother were here for that," I said as carefully as I could.

Sandy leaned back in her chair, sighed and said, "So, now you not only want my help in expediting your adoption of a little girl who is deep in one of the biggest hot-button issues of our time but now you want me to help you bring her mother to this country as well?"

I just nodded and said simply, "Yes."

"Hal, what you are asking is…Alright, let's take this one step at a time here. Are you two going to adopt this girl together?" Rowena looked at me and looked at her, and I realized we had not even discussed that.

"Would that help?" I asked.

"Immensely. It is easier to sell this idea to the right people if a loving couple adopted a child rather than a single man. It would really help your case if you two were married. Have you thought about that?"

I looked at Rowena and was about to say something when Rowena spoke first, "Well, there's a problem with that too."

Sandy's leaned forward and said, "Now, what?"

"Well, we can't really get married here in Texas."

"And why is that?"

"Well…I used to be a man," Rowena answered.

I swear I could hear Sandy blink. Never before had I ever heard anyone's eyes make noise but this blink was like those big metal doors that the mall uses to close up shop. Sandy didn't say anything for what seemed like a minute, but then she smiled and said, "This is a joke right? Tell me this is a joke," Sandy looked at both of us and realized we were serious, "No, no, no. This is…I don't…I mean…really…really…"

I saw that she had lost her footing in the reality we had just presented her, so I tried to smooth things over. "Sandy, I know this is a lot to take in. But I really care for Shī, and I want to make this happen."

"Hal, do you realize that you have just handed me each and every issue that the Republican's stand against in this country all wrapped in one case?"

"I know it's a strange situation but…"

"…this is political Kryptonite. I mean I know that I am a Democrat and liberal, but Jesus Hal, this is too much."

"So, will you help us?" I asked, not knowing what else to say.

Sandy looked at both of us and said, "Let's start with the easiest thing first. Gay marriage is the one issue that Republicans know they have lost, so they aren't even fighting that anymore, so let's start there. We could probably do this in Austin."

"Well," Rowena interrupted Sandy, "we're not gay. I'm a woman."

We were about half way home when Rowena said, "Well, I think that went well."

I turned to look at her and then looked back at the road. "I just want to focus on the quinceñera if that's okay."

"She did agree to go to Shī's quinceñera. So, that's a plus."

When we got home, Shī was already home and sitting at my grandmother's kitchen table working on her homework. Rowena got out of the car and quietly walked up to behind Shī and said, "Hey, chica, how is my little feminista?"

Shī jumped up and hugged Rowena, "Rowena! I missed you so much. You are here for the summer?"

Rowena smiled and said, "Yes, I'm here to help you with your quinceñera because this is so out of Hal's league."

"That is so great. I've been reading all of the books you left me. I only have two left. I love them all."

"You read all ten?"

"Eight. I have two left to go."

Rowena looked at me in surprise. I shrugged and said, "What can I say, she reads better than me."

Rowena looked back down at Shī and said, "You are a little genius, aren't you?"

Shī blushed and said, "No, I just like to read."

"Spoken like a true genius. Come on, let's get some dinner."

"Can we get a botana?" Shī said knowing that we usually don't eat bad stuff until the weekend and today was Tuesday. She knew that Rowena was a pushover, and so she agreed. Shī looked at me knowing that with Rowena around, she would always get her way.

Saturday, May 30th. The last weekend before school let out and here I was going through the motions as Rowena ran around getting all of the last minute details down for the quinceñera. Rowena had rented the nice looking ballroom at the Echo Hotel, and she had gone all out with a crazy costume picture taking booth. A crazy mixed song where Shī and I would dance a pre-choreographed dance number and then the big surprise. Shī's mother was here, and we were going to unveil her at the opportune time. Sandy had come through and been able to get Gisela Zapoteca a temporary visa for two weeks here in the States. But our marriage and Shī's adoption were going to take time and skill. Her mother was Rowena's and my birthday gift to Shī. Besides the $100 gift card to Amazon, which I couldn't help but get her.

We decided against the church mass because neither of us were very religious, but the reception, which was about to start at 5 pm, was what really mattered, Rowena told me. Rowena had her two boys helping her set everything up. Me, I just waited in the back with Shī's mom, mostly silent because my K'iche was really bad and her Spanish wasn't that great. Gisela was a beautiful woman; I could see where Shī got her looks. Gisela was young. She was only twenty-seven years old. She had Shī when she was thirteen and her husband who had disappeared in Guatemala a few years was only thirty. More than likely he was dead, but we never talked about that. I was ten years older than her and yet she seemed so much older than her age. We mostly sat and occasionally smiled at each other. I wondered what she thought about me. I know Shī talked about me with her mother. Shī would call her every week and tell her everything about her life in K'iche, so I could never understand. But still, a single man taking in a thirteen-year-old girl was weird from anyone's perspective, even if he did rescue her. I loved Shī as a daughter, and I never saw her that way. But you can't explain that to people, so I don't even try.

"Hal," someone called for me.

I turned and saw Sandy standing there in a very nice black dress that had a drop-down V cut that allowed an ample of cleavage. She had her hair down, and she looked extremely hot. "How are things going with Mrs. Zapoteca?"

"Very well. We mostly nod and smile."

"Yeah, they told me she doesn't speak too much Spanish."

"No, I need Shī to translate, but that would ruin the surprise. Luckily, she knows just enough Spanish for her to understand what is going on here and Rowena knows just enough K'iche so that we could plan this surprise."

"Great. Can you talk?"

"Sure," I got up and we both walked out to the bar in the back of the hotel. We ordered a couple of whiskey sours and sat down at the bar.

"So, this is really nice. Rowena has done a great job."

"Yeah, she's amazing."

"How long have you two been together?"

"About two years. We got together right before I found Shī."

"Yeah, I read your book. I understand now. The whole trans thing. I get it."

"I don't see her that way anymore. I just see her as a woman."

Sandy took a drink from her glass. "I'm guessing you didn't tell her about us."

"Noooo. Are you kidding? I want peace in my house."

"I felt the daggers from her eyes when you guys were in my office. She definitely knows we have history. I mean it was ten years ago, but women can smell that."

"Yeah, but if there is one thing I have learned from one failed marriage is that there are some things best left untold."

"I don't know about that. I think if it was out in the open it won't come back to bite you in the ass later on."

I looked at her, and I saw something in her that I hadn't seen since we used to date all those years ago. It was desire. It scared me because she was still so hot, but, "Sandy, I can't. I love Rowena and us, you know, that would be very bad. I mean you, you're married with kids."

"Hal, I wasn't hitting on you. Calm down. It's just nostalgia, you know. What could have been?"

"What could have been is a dangerous thing? Always has been and always will be."

Sandy looked down at her glass and swirled the ice around,

"I'm happy with my life, don't get me wrong, but sometimes, you know…"

"Yeah, I know. But for the first time in a long time, I am happy with my screwed up life. I have a tranny fiancée, a refugee daughter, and two step kids who were fathered by that same fiancée. I couldn't have written a better story."

"But you did write it."

"It was more of a memoir than fiction."

"I know."

"And then, there's you. The politiquera who I dragged into this postmodern drama."

"Hey, Rowena is right. With you two I got the support of some of the most powerful LGBT groups in Washington, and I know have the support of the right Latino caucuses in Congress."

"Here's to unexpected successes in life," I said raising my virtually empty glass. Sandy clicked the glass with hers and we drank the last little bit.

"Well, Hal, it's always interesting with you."

"No problem, my pleasure. But seriously thanks for everything you are doing."

Sandy leaned in and kissed me, and I kissed her back for only a second until I realized what I was doing and backed out of the kiss. "That was old time's sake," she said and then walked away, "I'll see you in there. Oh, and one last thing. I got you guys a gift. I hope you like it."

"Really, what is it?"

"You'll see."

And she was gone. So I walked back to the room with Gisela and found her sitting with Jimmy, Rowena's oldest. "Jimmy," I said, "where's your Moppa?"

"She's inside with your mom and her mom yelling at the caterer."

"Okay, thanks." I went into the ballroom and found Rowena talking with our two moms, and I pulled her aside and said, "You have to get ready. Everyone will be here in thirty minutes."

Rowena nodded, and we both went out to the hotel room

we had rented. As soon as we entered, I grabbed her and kissed her hard. "I love you," I said and proceeded to take her there leaning over the wobbly little table.

The party went off and they did all of the things that quinceñera's do: the tiara, the cross, the bible wrapped in satin, the flower bouquet, the procession of the padrinos (people that gave us money to help put this shindig on), and then came the dance, which I did with Shī. It was a mixture of songs from various pop hits mixed in with some Spanish rock, and of course the traditional Mariachis at the end. Shī looked ecstatic. But the people in this room were people I really didn't know all that well. There were a few friends from Shī's school and then I saw that Curly kid who had a crush on Shī. I didn't like that kid at first, but lately he has been writing poetry to Shī, and she has been collecting it. The protective father in me wants to stomp that kid into dust, but I know that she needs that in her life. So I let it go, for now. Everyone seemed to be having fun. Sandy and her husband were sitting in the back. She had her two kids with her, but she was constantly texting through much of the procession. When it came time to reveal mine and Rowena's gift to Shī, I noticed a flood of cameras and reporters enter the ballroom.

I walked Gisela Zapoteca from the backroom to her daughter dolled up in that big pink and white fluffy quinceñera dress and matching quince shoes. Shī's eyes just widen like I had never seen, and she hugged her mother hard enough to almost break her in half. I could see the tears rolling out of Shī's left eye, and I almost felt like I wanted to cry myself. And as they exchanged words in K'iche, I heard in the back of the room camera flashes and Sandy talking to the reporters. Shī and her mother spoke by themselves for about an hour as people ate, drank, and danced to the over-priced DJ we had rented. Rowena laid her head on my shoulder and said, "You did good."

"I wish I could do more. I mean I wish we could keep Gisela here in the States."

"Didn't you hear Sandra talking earlier to the reporters?"

"No, what?"

"She is using Shī as the poster child for refugees. She is

advertising this quinceñera as a triumphant for immigrant rights. She is advocating for keeping her mother here in the U.S."

"Did she mention us?"

"No, she's not stupid. One battle at a time."

Someone said that everything in this world has already been photographed. There is nothing left to see. But that's not true. Not in the slightest. Because a camera captures moments and every moment is always new. Every second of every day brings a breath we have never breathed. A smell we have never smelled. A smile we have never seen. And even though our minds retain thousands of words that we reuse regularly every day, sometimes when they are spoken in a certain order, they say something new, something beautiful.

Shī stepped up to the mic to give her speech; it was that part of the night. I had no idea what she was going to say, but I knew she had been working on it for a week now. Writing in her notebook and then scratching it out and throwing it away. There were several crumpled up papers all around her room. But the moment was here, and she looked a little nervous.

"Hello, everyone, thank you for being here. This has been the best. Better than I could have imagined. I am lucky. More lucky than anyone I know. As you all know, I traveled from Guatemala to here and things happened from there to here. Things that no little girl should ever know. I didn't know what was going to happen when I would get here, but something extraordinary happened. I found kindness on a road that I thought for sure was hell. My story is like lightning striking a bottle. It doesn't happen until it does. But to me it did. You brought Mamma. That doesn't happen. Not to anyone. But here she is, and that is because of you, Hal. So I play this for you." Shī nodded toward the DJ, and he began to play a song. It took me a few seconds to recognize it, but then it was clear. It was "Shelter From The Storm" by Bob Dylan.

> *I was burned out from exhaustion, buried in the hail*
> *Poisoned in the bushes an' blown out on the trail*
> *Hunted like a crocodile, ravaged in the corn*
> *Come in, she said*
> *I'll give ya shelter from the storm*

Shī looked at me and mouthed the words, "I love you," and smiled.

Rowena hooked her arm in mine and buried herself in my side.

"Am I the woman?"

"Always," Rowena answered, "Always."

E(X)ILED

"Every revolution evaporates and leaves behind only the slime of a new bureaucracy."

—Franz Kafka

Luis M. sat outside the courthouse doors waiting. He had been waiting for over an hour now, and still the doors have never opened. There were several other people waiting in the hallways, some sitting, and some leaning against the walls staring at their phones probably on Facebook or Twitter or whatever cool social site was in fashion at the moment. The others stared blank into space or pre-occupied themselves with dozens of children running wild up and down the hallways. Luis M. didn't know how long these people had been waiting before he got here but he knew it had been a long time. Some he even thought looked like they had been here since before the place opened up.

Luis M. looked down at his hands and fought the urge to pull his phone from his pocket and check his email. He didn't want to miss his chance to get inside and clear this whole matter up. This whole thing had started two weeks ago...

It was a morning like any other. Hot. Humid. And all around the same as any other day in blistering South Texas. But on this particular day before even his alarm went off, he heard a knock on his front door. It was steady and insistent like a woodpecker maybe, but this was much more forceful. Luis M. slowly made his way out of bed and over to the door. He opened it to see two men dressed in black suits, white shirts, and black fedora hats with dark shades and white skin to contrast all of the darks. It was odd because no one wore suits in this Valley, it was just too unbearable, but here they were, not even sweating a drop.

The guy on the right spoke first, "Luis M.?"

"Yes," he answered.

"You are under arrest. Step aside," the guy on the left said as he pushed by a stunned Luis M.

Baffled Luis M. said, "What do you mean? What have I done?"

The two guys didn't answer, they just looked around his apartment, tossing books off of shelves, smashing plates and glasses, and rifling through his things. "Hey excuse me, I know my rights. You guys just can't come in and do this without telling me what I'm charged with."

The guy who was originally on the left stopped and came right up to Luis M.'s face and said, "Sir, you have no rights. You are under arrest. Now sit down or I will have to restrain you."

Luis M. didn't know what to do so he sat down on his sofa while they looked all over and after about twenty minutes, they had trashed his entire apartment. They took his flash drives, photos, books, and even some of his leftover calabaza con pollo he had been saving for lunch. When they were finished they turned to him, and the guy on the left said, "You will be getting a summons soon. I suggest you get a lawyer. These charges are quite serious."

"What charges?" Luis M. pleaded with them, but they were already out the door.

Luis M. didn't know what just happened. He didn't know who these guys were or what they wanted. Ultimately he decided to call the cops because this was some kind of strange home invasion, so he got his phone and dialed 9-11.

A woman's voice came on the line, "9-11. What is your emergency?"

"Yeah, some guys just came into my house and trashed it. They said I was under arrest, and then they just left."

"Mr. M., you are under arrest. Please don't call here again. You will be getting a summons at your place of employment. Go to work. And get a lawyer."

And that was it. She was gone, and the nightmare continued.

Luis M. got ready for work. Tried to pick up as much as possible but had to get to work. So he got his coffee and the one mug that wasn't broken and jumped in his car. He got to the bank where he worked as a loan officer, and everyone looked at him weirdly. He didn't know why but no one would look him in the eye. They kept their gazes down and continued about their business. Luis M. got to his desk and noticed that there was an official letter from the government sitting nice and neat on his computer keyboard. It was stamped and certified, all official like. Luis M. sat down at his desk and opened the letter. All it said was:

YOU HAVE BEEN EXILED.

Please go about your work. We will be contacting you for your court date.

P.S.-Get a lawyer

Luis M. was completely disturbed by this letter because it was written on official government letterhead from the Department of Homeland Affairs. He didn't know what it meant or what he was supposed to do so he decided to talk to his friend Mike De La Rosa in legal to see if he could help him out.

Mike was sitting at his desk with a stack of huge dot matrix printed binders of information on his desk. Luis M. knocked and said, "Mike, can I talk to you? I've been having a weird day."

Mike looked up at him and looked like he had seen a ghost. "Sorry Luis, can't talk to you. You are a marked man."

"But Mike, what do you mean? It's me, what's going on here?"

"Luis," Mike gestured to the corner of the ceiling, "I can't talk to you. Please just go and have a smoke break."

Luis M. looked up and saw a camera mounted in that corner. Something was really weird going on here, first because he didn't smoke and second, smoking was pretty much outlawed in this country. Luis M. went out to the side area where the last remaining smokers congregated and stood there waiting. A minute later Mike came out and pulled Luis aside to where no one could hear.

"Luis, what have you done? There are agents crawling all over the place. They put surveillance everywhere."

"I haven't done anything. I don't know what's going on. All I know is that these guys in suits came to my house, told me I was under arrest and then left. I came here and there was this letter saying that I had been exiled but that I should go about my work. What the hell is all this?"

Mike looking scared said, "You are not the first, and you won't be the last. They are cleaning house."

"Who? What are you talking about?"

"I can't explain anymore. They will know I have been gone. Go see Carlos Adama; he can help you."

"Who's that?"

Just then the side door burst open, and the same two agents burst out and grabbed Mike and pulled him inside. The one on the left turned to Luis M. as they were pulling Mike inside and said, "You are not allowed to collude with others."

"What? What are you talking about?" Luis M. pleaded again but once again he was gone.

Luis M. was extremely frustrated by this point, and so he did the only thing he could think of, he went back to work and did his job. He never saw or heard from Mike again. He was just gone, and still Luis M. had no answers as to what was going on. So, he finished his day and left to find Carlos Adama.

Luis M. found Carlos Adama easily enough because he had billboards all over town saying he could get anyone money for slips and falls, in English and Spanish. Carlos Adama was a lawyer who worked out of a barbershop deep in "Little Mexico," the Mexican side of McAllen. He had several clients in his waiting room that Luis M. could have sworn had killed people, and they were looking at him like he was Richard Ramirez. Adama's secretary was also the same girl who took the haircut appointments. She was around twenty, light brown skin, long flowing blondish-brown hair with a low-cut top and a short mini-skirt topped off with three-inch stilettos. Luis M. hoped that this lawyer's sleazy choice in a legal assistant didn't reflect his practice, but he was sure it did.

It only took about ten minutes before he was called back to Adama's office. Adama didn't look like a guy who had an office in a barbershop. He had a nice Brooks Brothers suit, well manicured, and expensive shoes. This guy looked like he belonged in that big black building downtown, not here.

Carlos looked at him and said, "So, you're the exile, huh?"

Luis M. sat down in front of his big mahogany desk and said, "Yes, that's me. What does all this mean?"

Carlos interlaced his fingers, leaned back in his leather chair and said, "Well, that's what we are going to find out. But I will be honest with you. No one who has kept their court date has ever been seen from again."

"What do you mean? They went to prison?"

"Prison? No, no, no. They are gone. Vanished. Deleted from the system."

"I don't understand. But I didn't do anything."

"Didn't you?"

"What do you mean? I haven't done anything illegal."

"This isn't about a crime you committed. This is about something much worse than that."

"And what is that?"

"Luis M. you are an exile. Your entire existence is a threat to the fabric of society."

"But why?"

"Have you ever heard of homo sacer?"

"No. What is that?"

"That is an ancient Roman legal designation for someone who is both sacred and cursed at the same time. It was used for people that could not exist in society, but the government couldn't just outright kill them either. They were banned from society and yet deemed worthless by society, so anyone could kill them and they wouldn't be tried for murder, but at the same time, they couldn't be sacrificed for a cause either."

"That's confusing."

"That's you."

"I don't understand any of this," Luis M. said bursting out of his seat, "Can't anyone give me a straight answer."

"If things were that simple, you wouldn't need me."

"How many of your clients are exiles?"

"All of them."

"And how many have you gotten off?"

"None yet. They are all still waiting for their court date."

Luis M. was more frustrated than ever. This lawyer had done nothing but convolute the matter. Luis M. looked at Carlos and asked, "So, what do I do know?"

Carlos leaned in and said, "Wait for a court date and then call me."

"You're gonna represent me?"

"Sure, but I won't be there. I am just here to file paperwork."

"What do you mean? So, I just go to the courthouse by myself? Don't you need to mount a defense or something?"

"Luis, there is no defense."

Luis M. left Carlos Adama's office feeling more helpless than when he got there. There were no answers for him there but yet he knew he had to fight this. Somehow, there had to be a way. Luis M. searched the Internet, read several books on exiles, and went back time and time again to the courthouse to try and get answers but he was always turned away. He went back to the lawyer's office and pled with him, but Carlos would only tell him the same thing, there was nothing he could do. So, after two weeks of going about his life as an exile, he finally got his day in court. It was a letter presented on his desk, the same way he had received his exile letter. He was told to go to the courthouse and wait and so he did.

He waited for years and years and yet the line at the courthouse never seemed to get shorter. He waited for more years and the line never moved. It was after several more years that Luis M. decided to go home. He stood up feeling his legs wobbly because he had been sitting for years and waited to get his bearings. When he took the first step, it was difficult but then after awhile, the blood rushed back to his legs, and he began to walk faster and faster to the front door of the courthouse. The hundreds of people waiting for years like him, watched as he walked toward the doors. No one had ever left. It was a sight to see, and as he got closer to the big double doors a hush fell over the crowd. It was so silent that Luis M. had to turn and look to see if everyone was still there. They were. So he pushed on the door for it to open and it did. He opened the door and a blinding light filled his vision. The light caused Luis M. to close his eyes until they adjusted to the brightness of the sun. It was the first time he had seen daylight in years. His eyes burned for a few seconds and then he took a step outside. When he did all he saw were those two agents that had burst into his home all those years ago. They grabbed him by the arms and pulled him into a black SUV with tinted windows. They didn't say a word. They just drove and drove until they ended up at Boca Chica Beach.

The beach was completely deserted. Not a single living soul was around. They pulled him out. Took his shoes and told him to walk toward the crashing waves. Luis M. didn't want to, but these agents looked liked they wanted to kill him and he had a feeling that if he ran they would just shoot him dead, so he did as they asked. He walked until the cold water splashed over his feet and then one of the agents said, "Stop. Get on your knees." And so he did.

He heard the slide of the barrel being pulled back. The click of the hammer as it was locked in place and right before he heard the bang, something miraculous happened. Off in the distance, down the beach toward the Mexican side, he saw a flash of light and a huge puff of smoke. Something rose from the horizon on the beach. It was a rocket and what followed was a sonic boom. It was the last thing he felt before he closed his eyes and waited…and he waited…and he waited…and he waited…

www.ingramcontent.com/pod-product-compliance
Lightning Source LLC
Chambersburg PA
CBHW030411120726
47904CB00007B/2234